THE JOURNEY

SANSHLIAN SERIES: BOOK 2

FoxTales Press

DANI HOOTS

The Journey
Sanshlian Series, #2
Second Publication © 2020 FoxTales Press
Content and line edits by Justin Boyer
Cover Design Copyright © 2020 by Biserka Designs

First Publication © 2017 Dani Hoots
Content and line edits by Justin Boyer of
Bibliophile's Workshop
Formatting by Dani Hoots
Cover Design Copyright © 2016 by Dani Hoots

ISBN for paperback: 978-1-942023-46-3
ISBN for ebook: 978-1-942023-47-0

To Faye and Veronica, who stuck by my side throughout the entire process, and really, really want to read more.

Chapter 1

Everything froze. It was like a picture; one instant captured in all of time and space. Except for me, which was quite frustrating. I didn't follow the rules, or laws that tied me down to this world. Heck, now that I knew the truth about who I was, I wasn't bound by the laws of time anymore.

I was the daughter of Nygard, after all. A Sanshlian. An Illusionist. A being so powerful that no one could stop me.

At least, that is what the legend said. I honestly didn't feel powerful. I felt the same as I always had been. I didn't even know how to control my abilities the way that Nygard or Violet did. Not yet anyways.

As I looked around the room in the abandoned building, the room that held Nygard prisoner for so many centuries, I saw everyone. I saw Neil as he tried to summon Nygard back into the world, the generals as they held back David, Will, and my brother. Jack, standing next to me as I felt like my mind was about ready to explode. Voices entered my head, voices of all the Sanshlians that were killed in the war against Nygard. It was agonizing, as they all tried to reach out to me and get me to listen, their voices becoming louder and louder, overwhelming all my senses.

No wonder Neil said most who touch the door go insane. I felt as if I would break any minute, wanting to take Jack's gun and end it right then and there.

That's when it happened. Everything stood still, and I was the only one who could move—who could see what was going on. Time seemed to go nowhere when all the pieces were put into place. Everything made sense. The legend. The truth. The lies. Everything. The tale was finally completed, and I knew what I needed to do.

I needed to fulfill the prophecy. The one that was passed down among many generations; the one I would end. And that was what all the voices were telling me. That is what they wanted me to know.

The moment I realized that, the voices became quiet and only one was left—one that I knew would stay with me through the end. The one that was directing me, knowing exactly what I needed to do to end this all. I took a deep breath. I had to stop Neil and destroy Nygard once and for all.

There was no escaping my destiny now. I had to end this tale before it started again. And to do that, I didn't need to take out the sword. I just needed to use the book. Taking the sword out would only cause more trouble. My father on Garvner had it all wrong when he told us those stories when we were little. It was the book that was the most powerful thing, something only an illusionist could handle.

Peering around for what felt like a suspended moment in time, I saw Neil as he made his way to the book. He knew the tale better than any of us, as his family had passed it down for many generations. He probably even knew where in the book to look for ways of reviving Nygard, as his own ancestors had fought alongside him.

But now I had the voice of guidance in my mind and I knew how to stop Neil from doing anything. There was one thing I wasn't taking into consideration, and it was the fact he could read my mind. He would know what I was about to do.

Then I remembered: he didn't want to snoop inside my head, not when he thought it was being taken over by all the ghosts of the Sanshlians that had passed away. I had the advantage.

The statue of Nygard stood in the middle, a sword through the chest, just as the legend dictated. It appeared old, bearing the signs of passing time. It didn't hit me until then, but that was my father standing there, or at least my biological one. I would never truly know him, and he would only be a legend distorted through time.

Voices came back into my mind as I returned to reality, words that had been lingering in this place for so many years. They had been waiting for such a long time to have this legend fulfilled. They were eager to help; a little too eager. But of all the words, only one stood out from all the rest.

Hvas.

I peered around to find out what they meant, to what they were imploring me to do. That's when I saw him, my brother, break out of Tom's hold, and bolt towards the statue. I had to stop him.

"No!" I shouted as Rik ran towards the statue. "If you do that, you will—"

I jerked awake, sweating. I took a few breaths, peering around to realize I was in another standard quarters given to military personnel. Sighing, I realized it was just another dream of the last moments of my old life—the life I wished I could regain. I knew it was wrong to think such things, but I wanted to go back to being the Emperor's Shadow, for all this to be some kind of dream. This legend was nonsense, and I didn't want to be troubled by it any longer. Then there was the matter of Jack...

I rubbed my face with my hand, trying to forget about it all, and was still surprised to see someone else's hand as my own. Light milky skin, a contrast to my more olive skin in my past life. A year had passed since Rik pulled the sword out of the statue and it still was surprised me to see this person's skin instead of my own, although I had regained my "real" body before my idiot brother pulled out the sword. So I guess I wished I had just killed him the moment he stepped into the Imperial Palace. Then my life would have stayed less complicated:

I would have remained in my old body, I would have never found out I was an Illusionist of the Sanshlians, I would still kill people that disturbed the peace of the Empire. I would still be with Jack.

No, instead I was still in my quarters, thrown back into the past during the start of the uprising for the eventual creation of Pandronan Empire. And where in the universe was my quarters? Oh, that's right. On Valle, the Capital of the Second Republic. I was in the government that existed before the Pandroran Empire of the future. We were sent back in time exactly where my brother wanted to be.

Speaking of my brother, the universe knew I hated him. If he would have just listened, then none of this would have happened. A year had already gone by and I was still at a loss in what I needed to do to get back to Sanshli to defeat Nygard once and for all. Instead, I was stuck in this place where I least wanted to be. If I could have just gotten my hands on the book on Sanshli, none of this would have needed to happen.

Because I would have reversed time from the moment Nygard was frozen in stone.

That way Nygard's followers would have nothing to search for, and there would have never been a Pandronan Empire. The Second Republic would have ruled for many more millennia.

But no, my brother had to screw it all up by taking the sword out of the statue's hold. But I guess it wasn't his entirely his fault Father had told the story wrong. Father had believed that taking out the sword would defeat

Nygard. No, it would only release him, and anyone who pulled it out would get their wish granted. And I guess Rik's wish was to be sent back into time to destroy the Empire from ever gaining any control. Made sense, since he blamed the death of Father and his wife on the Empire.

And why would the sword grant any wish? Because Violet couldn't finish defeating Nygard with the book, because she had used most of her power to encase him in the stone and keep him safely resigned to Sanshili. The rest of her energy was expended, of course, in sending me into the far future where this entire ordeal began. So it wasn't the sword in fact that granted the wish then, but Nygard himself being freed. So it was up to me to defeat him and Violet orchestrated everything to line up in the right sequence for that to happen. I could have called upon lost spirits to help me. That was what the voices were for. They were trying to help me. I only figured it out too late. From there, I had to start from scratch, and I would figure it out in the end. Just as I always have.

If everything had gone smoothly, I should have just been able to go straight back to Sanshli, and reverse all this. Well, I couldn't because when I tried to search for it with a telescope, it was gone. It was hidden with magic so it didn't exactly follow physics like we knew it. David had helped me with the search and he had no answer as to how that was possible either. So the search for Sanshli begins anew.

Standing up and stretching, I pulled my blonde hair

back with a ribbon. I was still in Myra's body, which I guess was really my own. It was still difficult to fathom one of the least weird things to happen after the event. It was strange to think my old body had not been my own, but a decoy. I was never truly Arcadia this entire time, she was just some made up person used to hide my existence from Nygard. My father knew that on Garvner, but he had always treated me like his daughter. I wondered what life would have been like if he was still alive, if he hadn't been killed. Would he have told me the truth? Would he have explained everything that was going on in time? Whatever, I would make do with what I had. There was no point of thinking about hypothetical situations.

Looking back down at my hands, I frowned. I still had that damn mark on my wrist from the Kamps. How, I'm still not entirely sure. Probably to remind me of what I was fighting for. Freedom. Either way, I still covered my hands with gloves. It was the only thing I could do to cope with all that had happened. It was the only way I could forget all the blood that I had shed.

I changed into my uniform, a star and crossed swords embroidered on the sleeves. It was something I laughed at every time I put it on. Here I was wearing the symbol of the Second Republic. Ironic, as I had fought so hard against those who tried to bring back the Republic, killing so many. But now I had to serve as one of them. "Had to" was the key word there, I never wore this symbol. I just woke up here, under the Second Republic's flag. It wasn't like I could run away either. Zipping up my jacket, I headed to work.

Venturing down the corridors, I made my way through the Capitol Building on Valle. It was still weird to think I was here and not in the New Capital's Palace on Anosira. I felt as if someone would shoot me at any second, but none of them knew the truth, and how could they? I didn't exist for another two hundred years. I hadn't killed all those men yet—the Pandronan Empire hadn't even gained control. The Second Republic reigned now.

As I put my hand on the control panel to open the sliding door, I took a deep breath and concentrated. Now that I learned I was an Illusionist, I knew that I had some types of powers. If I concentrated, I could hear what the walls were saying. It was weird, and they told me that there were people around, where the computers were located, and what the weather was like outside. All I wanted to do was make sure a certain someone was in the room before I entered.

And he was.

I entered the control room. Screens posted all the whereabouts of different military forces, mostly battling minor terrorist groups, rebellions, that sort of thing. The Empire was just starting to come into formation, in the form of a loosely organized enemy faction, so I wouldn't quite consider it the beginning of a full-fledged war yet. My brother assigned me to watch over things, making sure they went by smoothly. He didn't trust me on the front-end of war strategy, or on my own. I told him I'm better in the field, I could get a lot done on my own but he didn't care. He still didn't believe in me. I wondered why.

A shaggy brown-haired gentleman, the man I made sure was in there, already stood over the officer manning the screens, making sure they were doing their job. If there was anything wrong, then the men examining the screens came running to us and we dealt with the problem. I hated the job, there was a lot of sitting around required, but there wasn't anything else I could do. Not with the way they treated me. They still saw me as a threat and regarded me as a prisoner. Though, I couldn't blame them, now could I? I had betrayed them, was setting them up to all be slaughtered. I wouldn't trust myself either.

The man glanced over with his sweet green eyes that always seemed honest enough. His rugged face made him even more handsome, but I would never let him know that. David would take it too much as a compliment than just a statement, even though it wasn't his actual body. It was Lance Greel's, one of the head generals for the Republic before the fall. I wasn't the only one having to get used to a new body. It made me feel a little better about everything. Just a little.

When we were thrown back into the past, I found that my brother, David, and Will all had new bodies, their mind or soul being thrown into the bodies of those who played a key role in the Second Republic at the start of the war. Where Jack, Neil, and the generals were, I had no idea. I presumed they were on Anosira, but I wasn't "allowed" to go search for them, as my brother didn't trust me farther than he could spit. As for Jack, I didn't know where he could be, or if he was even thrown in the past along with us.

So yeah, I was stuck with Rik, David, and Will. Luck was always on my side.

Though, out of everyone here, David, who was now Lance, was the only one I trusted would tell me the truth. We would play games with each other, the mental kind, as I was too sick of card games still. We would battle verbally, never letting a lie escape our mouths, yet played with words to make the truth stay hidden. It was almost like jesting, in a way. An understanding that we each had about the other. No one else here trusted me, and deep down, Lance (David) didn't trust me either. But he wanted to, and that is what I knew I could use in this time of disorientation. As long as I kept that part of him in my favor, I could escape here one day, if need be.

And I presumed that day would be sooner rather than later.

Because let's be honest, I couldn't stay here. I needed to figure out where Sanshli had gone, and put an end to this madness, and only I could do that. My brother didn't let me work on that, so I had to get away from him and finish this journey once and for all. I couldn't keep living this life. And I had a feeling people around me could detect my anxiousness, so it was to my benefit to act before they tightened the leash around my throat.

"Myra." Lance noticed as I stepped inside the room, a look of surprise was apparent on his face. His eyes were gigantic and shifting towards the screens as if looking for something. "It's not your shift yet."

We decided it would be best to use our new names, not to arouse suspicion from those who lived during this time, not that it would matter what they called me. I didn't belong in this time, and neither did I belong in the future. I belonged centuries earlier, not that it mattered. It just made me feel as if I didn't belong anywhere. But I went by my real name and so did everyone else. It took a while for everyone to get used to, but no one even noticed the changes in personality, which we were thankful for.

"I woke early and decided to put my time to use." And I hated being left out in fear that my brother would do something stupid again.

Lance stepped closer, out of hearing of the soldiers, and whispered. "Dreams again?"

I watched as he studied me, worrying about the nightmares I had been experiencing for such a long time. It was silly, really, as my nightmares were never a problem for me. I learned to live with them, just as I learned to live with everything that has happened to me. I couldn't help it, I wanted to survive and to do that I moved past everything in time, of course with much effort spent. But Lance was different, he tried to care, one of the first people to do such a thing. He made it clear why he cared, and I clarified that Jack was the only person for me. But he still treated me with kindness. He could never take a hint.

"Don't worry about it," I replied.

He sighed, then turned back to the screens. "I think

you should go back and rest. Maybe do some training or something."

Lance usually liked it when I came early, then he got to spend more time with me. It was no joke, he actually told me that once. I didn't respond. Although between him, my brother, and Will, I could tolerate spending time with David. However, I still didn't like it. I would never tell him that, it would crush his little heart. So him telling me I should leave only brought up more suspicion. Something was going on that I wasn't meant to see.

"You want me to leave? Why?" I questioned, keeping my eyes on his averted gaze. My brother had to be contemplating doing something I found disagreeable. That's always when Lance would give me this dismissive shrug-off. Unfortunately, my brother did many things I didn't agree with and it surprised me I hadn't shot him in the heart yet, though that was because I had two people always stopping me from doing so.

"Myra, please, just go," Lance repeated, his tone low.

I shoved him out of my way, easily might I add since this was David we were talking about, and looked at the screen. A bunch of men were being gathered together in legions, training, being given orders to attack—an attack that did not need to happen, one that would lead to killing innocent lives. Because, if I knew my history right, which I did, the planet they would attack hadn't yet made any treaty with the Pandronan Empire. In fact, it wouldn't happen for another two years. This attack had no logical motive, only to instill fear into the citizenry of Ttkas for the Second Republic's benefit.

"I'm going to kill him," I stated as a matter of fact. No anger in my voice, which always made people around me fear the words even more.

Lance grabbed my arm. "Arcadia, don't make me stop you again."

I glared at him for calling me by my old name in front of the workers that surrounded us—not that they would notice. They acted like they didn't notice our fight, knowing not to get involved with superior officers, which was a smart move on their part. Minions should know their place, I was glad at least these officers knew that.

"I won't hurt him, I just need to talk to him about his idiotic tactics." I grinned innocently. "That's all. I mean, someone has to do it, since the two of you just serve him blindly, right?"

He eyed me, sighing as he let go of my wrist. He always gave in, though I wasn't sure if it was because he trusted me or because if I wanted to do something to my brother, he wouldn't be able to stop me. No one could stop me if I wanted him dead. Though the reason I have kept him alive was beyond me. I spun on my heel and departed towards his majesty's throne room.

Chapter 2

As I walked down the corridors towards where I knew my brother was working, I tried to slow down my rapidly beating heart through deep breathing exercises. It worked, sort of. My mind was still full of anger, that my brother would stoop so low as to hurt innocent people just because he thought he was right. He wanted to defeat the Empire before they rose, but by doing this he was no better than any Emperors to come. He was making the Second Republic into an Empire.

And yet everyone around him followed him blindly. It was pathetic, sickening really. No wonder the Second Republic was doomed to fail. They had no sense of democracy, and no sense of unity. They didn't know what they were fighting for if they went along with my brother's tactic so willingly.

I shouldn't care, it wasn't any of my business, but after being treated like a criminal for killing people whom they ordered me to assassinate, it made me pissed. He was no better than I was, probably worse. I had been under orders, trying to stop those who brought danger to the Empire I served. He was just killing others out of fear of the future, a future that may not even happen. Pulling out the roots before the plant even grew. It was an excellent tactic, yes, but was it moral?

So, even with his fear nestled in his head, my brother got the position he always dreamed of, not just some simple general like David, Will, and I all were. Rik was the Chancellor of the Second Republic, Wesley Atkins, or what I liked to call Emperor. He did whatever he wanted instead of following the true meaning of democracy. And yet everyone seemed okay with it, the representatives, the senators. Ironic, him becoming the monster he swore to destroy. Funny thing was, Neil would have never stooped as low as Wesley just did.

Well, maybe. He used me to find Sanshli so he could try to resurrect Nygard.

It was a lengthy walk through the Capitol Building. It felt weird, but I held my head up high as I usually did. I didn't sulk; I didn't let my eyes turn away from my goal. That never changed about me, and I would never let it. It was my strength, not letting others put me down, nor step on me. I was stronger than them, and I made sure they knew that.

I had to block out the whispers in the walls around me. I could feel everything that was going on in the building and it was overwhelming at times like these. If I was emotional, which wasn't often, then the intuition and the connection I had to the surrounding material grew. It was like the madder I got, the more I could use my powers. I didn't like this since I fought, and solved problems better with a level head. But this power of the Illusionists, it was something different, something I didn't have complete control over. The only thing I could really do at the moment was trust my intuition and let the walls speak to me, as if they were a living thing. It came in handy in evading my brother or even Will. And to find Lance (David) when I needed to hide behind him. He always stood up for me, even though he knew I was guilty of whatever it was I was being harassed about.

I shoved the doors open to his office, making as big of an entrance as I could. I wanted my brother to see my fury, to see how pissed I was at him for what he was about to do, for him to think twice before committing such an immoral act. The doors swung open, slamming into the wall. I hoped they left holes where the elegant doorknobs hit the wall, or at least chipped something. If I could only be so lucky.

Two senators sat in the chairs, meeting with Wes the magnificent, which is what I sarcastically called him since that was how he was treated and how I was sure he saw himself being. From what I recalled, the two senators were Tobor and Valmar of the Niot system. I didn't care one wit about them. Many of the senators backed him in the attacks he made towards what he said were Imperial-friendly planets. He may get them to believe his lies, but I knew the truth. I knew he was corrupt, scared, and a weakling. Only weak people attacked planets that contained innocent people. I would know, I had seen it all happen before.

Wesley's eyes widened as he saw the fury that filled me. He didn't expect me to find out so soon, I guessed. He should have known better, I was the Emperor's Shadow after all. That position came with a lot of work and a lot of learning how to stay one step ahead of the enemy, and right now I felt that my brother was the enemy more than Nygard truly was.

"I have a bone to pick with you, Wes." I would have yelled but years of training by Neil, the Emperor I once served, made me hold my composure in front of guests. Damn my background and damn him for teaching me to be proper. So many times have I wanted to kill his guests, but he would stop me and scold me for being so childish. It wasn't my fault they were all idiots.

Wesley turned to the senators. "I think we should pick up our meeting later. Please, let my staff know if there is anything you need. I will call upon you later this evening."

The senators nodded and left, but not without staring at me on their way out. They probably had every reason to. As a general, I didn't have the authority to demand the Chancellor like this. A reaction like the one I had was suspicious, but they had no right to ask. That's what I loved about the position I was in, I didn't have to worry about questions. I didn't glance at them but kept my icy glare fixed on Wesley, my brother. I had a feeling that he feared what I would do the moment the doors closed, and he was right, I wanted to beat the living daylights out of him, to teach him a lesson for once. But I wouldn't, because not only would that not be proper, but I was sure they would shoot me a few times, stabbed even, and then left outside for the birds to pick at my flesh. That was if I was lucky.

The doors shut behind me.

Wes was the first to talk, shuffling papers as if he didn't fear me standing there this whole time. I could see right through it, though. "Looks like Lance did a horrible job at keeping secrets from you. I should have figured as much."

I gritted my teeth. "Or maybe he knew it was wrong and was letting me know the truth so I could stop it."

"No, I think it has to do with the way he feels about you." Wes tried to see what reaction I would have from his comment, but I didn't give him the pleasure. I learned how to hide my emotions a long time ago.

"And yet you let him make a fool out of himself by ordering him to watch me. You know he tries so hard for me to notice him. And you stand by and make fun of him. Not to mention you let him do your dirty work. If you want to deal with me, do it yourself."

He shrugged. "Who else would watch you? Me? Alan? I don't want to deal with you and Alan always threatens to kill you after a second of being near you."

He had that right. Will, who was now Alan, certainly made it clear that he wanted my head on a silver platter every time I saw him. It didn't bother me, though, he couldn't take me down even if he tried. I hadn't met a person who could, although Tom came close. Unfortunately, Tom always had one weakness I could exploit. One kiss on his lips and he would forget about any fight that was going on. It was sad, but something I had no problem in using against him. Where in the universe he was at this moment, I had no idea. I presumed he would have been thrown back in time just like the four of us, but none of us had run across him or anyone else that had been in the cave. By my calculations, Tom, Laura, Pete, and Neil should be somewhere during this time. And Jack.

"I guess that is true."

"So." He tapped his finger together. "I believe this conversation is at a close."

I pounded my fist on the table. "Damn it, Wes! I am not done talking to you about this! Don't think just because you hold the title of Chancellor that I will treat you like one. You are no Chancellor, you are just a pathetic boy who can't stand not having his way!"

He glared at me, trying to threaten me with his eyes. It wouldn't work, I wasn't that easily deterred. They had threatened me way too many times in my life to ever take them seriously. Mostly because ninety-nine percent of the time they were empty threats. The other one percent, well, there was a reason my fast healing abilities came in handy.

Wes grabbed some papers and straightened them out. "The deed has been done, there is no going back."

I shook my head. I couldn't believe what I was

hearing, after everything that had happened. After all that we went through to find Sanshli, he responds by making more destruction for innocent families across the galaxy. Innocent families just like ours once was. "I should just kill you, brother, the galaxy would be a better place. Or, at least, I know I will be damn happier."

He smiled, as if he enjoyed me telling him I wanted him dead, though I said it more often than not. "And what's stopping you? Because you keep saying you want to kill me, but you never seem to act on it. It's interesting, really."

"I promised Lance I wouldn't. Besides, Father would come back to haunt me if I did such a thing," I paused. "Although I think he might agree with me if I did. I think he would want to see you dead, if you weren't his son."

Laughing, Wesley stood up and came out from around his desk. He stood tall, I supposed it came with the position. He had short curly brown hair now and his eyes were just a different shade of green than they were before we were thrown into the past. He stepped up to me, looking down at me as if I was just some little girl. I glared at him, not letting him have the superior feeling he always wanted.

He whispered, "As if all the lives you have taken over the years hasn't left you drowning in blood."

I smiled, knowing he would bring up my past once again. It was where the conversation always went, where he thought my weak point was a means he could use to elevate himself and cast me out as a demon. "All of mine had a reason to die. What you are doing is pure genocide."

"It's not genocide when Ttkas will become the leading army for the Empire," he explained as if that was all he needed to start a full-on massacre. He was wrong, even I could see that. I doubt even Nygard would do such a thing.

"But that hasn't happened yet! You are killing innocent lives!" I exclaimed.

He stepped closer, our faces inches apart. "If I stop the war from happening, then I will save lives, don't you see that?"

I shook my head. "No, I just see a mad man corrupt with power. Nothing more, nothing less."

He stepped away, looking out the window down at the city of Valle. He was silent for a moment, as if gathering his thoughts. He knew I was right, had to know I was right. There was no logic in the things he was doing, there was no logic in any of this.

"I'm sorry you feel that way, but you know I'm right," he said. "If I destroy all the defenses on Ttkas before the Empire can use them, I will stop the war from escalating like it did. We wouldn't have to worry and we could just pluck the rest of the Empire like the weed that it is."

I looked at him in disgust. My brother had turned heartless after Amanda had been killed on Ttkas. I figured he would warm back up, realize that in order to defeat Nygard, in order to bring back Amanda and the life he wanted, he had to do this fairly. But he never did. Now he wanted to erase Ttkas completely off the map. I wondered if it had anything to do with Amanda being killed there, as that was where Tom, one of the generals I served Neil with, had shot her. He shouldn't be going after the planet but after Tom himself. I'm sure he was around somewhere in this time. We weren't exactly sure since everyone changed bodies. But Tom was the one who killed Amanda, just to get to me. I felt a little guilty, but she knew what she was getting herself into. She knew the risks. And so did Rik.

"You shouldn't let revenge rule you," I stated. "It will only bring you pain and suffering."

"You haven't lost someone close to you Myra, you don't know what it's like."

He kept saying those words, but he didn't know how wrong he truly was. I had lost our Father, and not only that, I had been thrown into the Kamps after his death, a place where I practically had to kill other kids like myself to survive. Even after all that, I never got the revenge I wanted—I was always stopped by Neil. Not only that, but I had lost Jack the moment we were sent into the past.

And I still hadn't found him.

"We don't know where Neil and the rest of the Imperials are. For all we know, they will go about a different tactic. You can't destroy Ttkas when you know the other side has different players too." I tried to reason with him, but I knew it was no use. Revenge had clouded his judgment, and he wouldn't come back from it. I didn't know why I kept trying, but here I found myself again. Arguing with a brick wall, a very dense brick wall with no way of breaching his sanity. That was if the grief hadn't exterminated every bit that made him rational.

"We know exactly where they are, they are on Anosira," he said.

"But neither of you have made a proper move against each other so we can't know for certain," I commented. None of us knew the truth of where they were, we had only assumed. I had been waiting for some clear message from someone, but nothing at this point. Either they were being quiet, waiting for me, or they had no more use for me. It felt strange, as I was a tad disappointed that Neil wouldn't come for me, to either help him or torture me for betraying him. Either way, I felt unwanted, cast out of the life I once knew.

"Are you curious so you can go back to them, or are you curious because you want to know if Jack is with them?"

I raised my eyebrow. "Why do you think I would go running back to them?"

He shrugged. "It's just something you would do. You are the Emperor's pet after all."

"*Was* is a better word. I am no longer the Emperor's Shadow. He made that clear on Sanshli. He was just using me, knowing who I was before I even knew." Which was strange. He had been waiting all that time for the prophecy to be fulfilled, for my Sanshlian heritage to be awoken so he could revive Nygard, who all his family once served.

"We will see about that," he commented as he placed his hand on the table. "Now, what are we going to do with you?"

I narrowed my eyes. "What do you mean?"

"You don't really think I will let you cruise around when you keep threatening to stop me from attacking Ttkas, now do you? Lance will watch you until everything is executed, just like old times."

"You don't trust your own sister?" I asked.

"Ha! I have never trusted you. Not after finding out you had sold yourself to the Empire."

"You always bring the Empire up in our conversations, you really do fear them, don't you? You are afraid you won't win this and everything will be for nothing." I watched him carefully, noting that never met my eyes when we spoke like this. "That Amanda's death will be for nothing."

"Just shut up, Arcadia." He never used my new name. He could never bring himself to realize I was a Sanshlian. That I was never his sister. "You do not understand what pain I have gone through."

"No, you are right, I do not understand what it's like to have my life ripped out from underneath me, undergo years of torture, and then to be called a monster by the entire galaxy."

We held each other's gaze when suddenly the door opened and Lance stepped in. He looked a little worried, probably thinking he would find me with my hands at Wesley's throat. He should know better by now that I had stopped trying to actually kill him. Someone always came in and ruined the fun. Usually Alan.

I turned back to Wesley. "You are out of control, let

Lance and Alan help you."

He slammed his fist against his desk. "No! I will not be treated like I am crazy! I'm doing this for the good of all the people."

I saw the look on Lance's face. He knew as well as I that Wesley had overdone it this time, but I knew Lance wouldn't stand up against him. He would just follow Wesley even if it was into his own grave. Pretty soon it would be.

I turned and headed for the door. Lance followed. There wasn't anything I could do to stop him, I had to just accept it. "Keeping telling yourself that, Rik. Lies become truth if you say them enough times."

With that, I left him alone to ponder what I said and headed to my own quarters, chuckling to myself over the strange turn of events this time switcheroo had forced on us.

Chapter 3

I was quiet as I walked down the corridors with Lance. I knew whatever I would say, he would take Wes's side of it. He always did. For some reason, he and Alan followed Wes' commands. They thought I was wrong for following Neil, but at least I had my reasons. At least I accepted why I did it—I did it to survive. But then I found out the only reason I survived was because Neil had used me for his own devices. To think if I wasn't the daughter of legend, I would have been killed after I tried to assassinate the Emperor in the Kamps. Interesting how things played out.

So I had nowhere to run to. I couldn't stay here, not without killing my brother. If I ran to Anosira, I would find Neil and he would more than likely want me dead, as I had already led him to Sanshli. Then again, I could be wrong. He might still need me to find the book he wanted so badly. I doubt he got to keep it when we were all thrown back in time. I didn't know how to find that book since the planet had disappeared from where it was. Lance and I tried to find it again, so we could get the book before Neil did, but we never found it. After a while Wes made us stop using resources to find it, as it was no use according to him. I didn't care what Wes said and wanted to keep looking, but Lance was stupid and followed Wes' orders. I was pretty much winging it on my own now.

Well, that wasn't completely true.

Lance and I arrived to my quarters and entered. The room was bleak as always; I didn't know what to do to make it feel more like home because I never knew what it was like to be at home or even to have a home. I learned to always be on the run, ready to go at a moment's notice. But now that I was stuck here under my brother's close supervision, I noticed these things about myself. I was getting cabin fever, and I hated it.

Heading over to my dresser, I pulled out the pocket-watch Father had given me the last time I had seen him alive many, many years ago. Well many years later from this perspective of time. It somehow journeyed through time with me, for which I was glad. It was something I could look at to remind myself of both my Father and of Jack. It kept on ticking, as if nothing had ever happened. I wished I could be like the watch, an unchanging thing, not worrying about change or progression through time. Maybe once I had thought of myself like it, but now I wasn't too sure that the description fit.

"Still works," Lance stated as he stepped up behind me. I didn't pay him any attention even though he stood close. I wasn't sure if he would place his hand on my shoulder or not. He had tried to make a couple of advances, but I explained to him I didn't fall in love with my captors. He didn't have a good retort to that, as I was right—I wasn't here on my own free will.

"Just as always." I snapped it closed and placed it in my pocket. "So did you come to see if I would hurt Rik?"

He ran his hands through his hair, as if ashamed he didn't trust me still. I didn't blame him, I didn't trust me either. "You sounded like you two were going to kill each other again."

I shrugged with a slight smile. "Just some harmless sibling squabbles. You know how those can be."

He laughed. "Harmless is an interesting way to put it, last time I heard you two arguing like that I found you at his throat."

Which instance he was referring to, I didn't know. There had been so many before this.

"I didn't attack him this time, I learned my lesson the first few times."

"Which was?" he questioned, as if I was a child that couldn't quite learn her lesson.

"To not attack him or Alan will shoot me. Again. Took a few days to heal last time. He shot to kill, even though you both know I'm right."

"Myra..." Lance began.

"What do you want me to say, Lance? He's an idiot

and you know it! He's killing innocent lives in the name of justice. None of those people have done anything wrong!" I promised myself I wouldn't get in this argument with him again, but alas I did anyway. Something about him made me want to talk everything out. I hated it.

"You are one to talk," he added. It was always their counter-response, as if I was some kind of monster. Maybe I was, maybe that is why I could see the monster inside my brother. I knew monsters all too well.

"Everyone I have ever killed has deserved it. Rik is planting evidence against governments on planets for an excuse to strengthen the Republic's hold. Who's the monster now, eh?"

Lance grabbed my hand. "He is just trying to settle the score. You know he isn't thinking clearly."

I pulled my hand away and shook my head. "How long are we going to let him make the wrong choices? How long are we just going to sit here and do nothing?"

"Myra, settle down," he calmly ordered, placing his hands on my shoulders.

I shoved him backwards, a little more violently than I meant to. "Don't you dare tell me to settle down!"

Suddenly I felt cold water rush into my face. I gasped, coughing on the drops I had breathed in. Damn Lance. I glared at him. An interesting thing happened when we were all thrown into the past, Will, David, and Rik not only changed physically, but also had gained the ancient powers of the Sanshlians. I already had the power of the Illusionists, which I didn't have a good grasp on yet, but the other three had elemental powers, like most of the Sanshlians had before Nygard. Lance had the ability to control water. I must have left a glass out because he needed water from somewhere to use it. He wasn't as powerful as the legends were, since most Sanshlians could create elements out of thin air whereas Lance and the others needed something concrete to work their powers. They could move the elements already existing around them, not create them from nothing.

I should have been more careful where I left things.

I wiped the water out of my eyes. "You ass."

"You wouldn't calm down," he defended, a little scared I would retaliate against him. This wasn't the first time he had splashed me with water. I remembered when the three of them realized they had powers. And, of course, Will used his against me for the better part of the day.

I rolled my eyes as I went to the restroom to dry myself off. Shutting the door behind me, knowing he would follow me in like a little puppy, I sighed. He was always such an overly conscientious person sometimes.

"He's a pompous, arrogant asshole. Why can't I kill him?" I looked into the mirror. Some, well actually, a lot of people would have thought I was inside talking to my reflection in the mirror like this, only when I stared in the mirror long enough, I didn't see my reflection. I saw my Mother's. Violet's. That's right. One of her last spells connected to the sword dealt with me being able to see her until it was all finished. Talk about a buzz kill, having one's Mother around constantly. It would be fine if she would actually train me on how to be an Illusionist, but of course that never happened.

I didn't quite understand how she could do it, appear before me like this when she wasn't alive any longer. All I knew was that the first time I looked in a mirror after waking up in this era, she appeared and I almost screamed. Almost.

"Because it could bring disorder to everything. Your task is to bring order. Your task is to destroy the evil and restore the good," she explained. I was the only one who could see and hear her, I was the only one who could talk to her. I didn't necessarily need to speak out loud, speaking out loud just made me feel better. I didn't speak out loud when people were near. Right now, I didn't think Lance could hear me, or at least I hoped he was not eavesdropping on what might sound like a maniac talking to one's self.

"It has been a year, and I have gotten nowhere," I explained. "Wes doesn't let me out of anyone's sight. I need a change of pace. I hate waiting like this."

"Don't worry, your task will come soon. Be ready."

"I *am* ready," I said with surprising sternness. I have had it with waiting, I wasn't a patient person by nature, not when I knew I could end something now, and I had enough faith in myself to bring the end of this war.

"We will see about that. Have you been practicing shielding your mind?" She looked at me with those purple eyes of hers. They were lovely and her light hair only enhanced them even more.

The one and only thing she had taught me thus far

was how to protect my mind from those who could read it. Only let someone read what I wanted them to read. It would come in handy. "I have. Just don't know if it will work until I meet someone who can read minds," I argued.

"Fair enough. Now, calm down. You're our last hope, Myra."

I dropped my head, taking my eyes away from her to organize my thoughts before speaking. "I already told you I don't like it when you put that kind of pressure on me."

Especially since I wasn't quite sure what I needed to do to end this curse, as I called it. I knew I needed to find Sanshli and the book that Nygard had and then use it to destroy Nygard. Somehow, at least...

"I'm sorry but you need to be ready to face the facts. Only you can win this."

"Win what?" I questioned. "I don't even understand why we were brought back at this point in time. What is there to beat? The Empire? Rik, Wes, whoever he is, is doing a splendid job at that already. What else is there to do? I need to get to Sanshli and finish what you wanted me to finish."

"Patience, daughter. The time will come when you will understand it all."

"Can't you just tell me? It would make my life a lot easier," I countered.

She shook her head. *"I'm sorry but I can't."*

"Fine, just fine," I mumbled.

A knock sounded at the door. "Myra, are you okay?"

Lance's voice came through the barrier.

"I'm fine," I grabbed what I came into the room for. A towel to wipe up the water he had thrown at me. And something else... "Why do you ask?"

"It's just that I can hear you talking to yourself."

So he could hear me. Now I knew. "Just getting my frustration out. I will be out in just a minute."

I grabbed the vial I hid under the sink and swallowed the liquid. It was an antidote to the narcotic I was about to place on my lips. I couldn't go along with this any longer, even if Violet insisted I stay here. I would knock out Lance and run away. Honestly, I could knock Lance out by fighting him, but this way I didn't have to worry about hurting him too much. Sometimes I got carried away and though I didn't care for him, I didn't want to deal with that mess. I opened the tube of lipstick and put it on my lips, careful to keep it on the outside of my mouth.

There was one day I was able to leave my leash Wes gave me and venture out into the city for an hour or so. No one noticed, but for some reason after that, security got even tighter. I was probably because that was when Wes started digging his own grave by attacking innocent people. While I was out, I found this tube of lipstick. Not in a good part of town, if I might add. I knew I would need it sooner or later to escape.. Years of training taught me that. Always plan for everything ahead of time. Premeditated attacks always work best.

I had to get out of here, I couldn't't stand it anymore, even if Violet didn't want me to. I needed to see if my suspicion about the Empire was correct, that the rest of the people on Sanshli were part of the soon-to-be Pandronan Empire faction. So today was the day I got to test out my lipstick.

I opened the door and smiled. "Better now."

"Let out all of your frustration?" he questioned, glancing at the light shade of pink my lips were now. He said nothing about it, but I noticed a little bit of a blush on his cheeks.

"Yup," I looked at the clock. I didn't want to do it here, I wanted to be closer to an exit. My quarters were far from any exit, Wes made sure of that. "I take it you will be watching me for a while. Mind if we hit the training room?"

He raised an eyebrow. "I'm not going to be your dueling partner, I'm not that stupid."

"No, I'll just train using the bag. Going against you doesn't help my fighting, only tests my patience."

"Gee, thanks," he remarked.

Shrugging, I added. "I can't help it if you lack physical training, I tried to help you."

"Yeah, yeah," he gestured to the door. "Let's just go already."

I was quite surprised that Lance let me go to the training room. I thought for sure he was smarter than that. Then again, he knew if I wanted to get away, nothing would stop me.

We entered the training room. Only a small group of men were in there.

"Leave us," I ordered. They gave me one glance and

left without a word. Good dogs always obeyed authority and men like them were all the same throughout history.

"It surprises me you can still order around whoever you want with such authority. People in this timeline fear you as much as they did in the future," Lance commented.

"I really doubt that, but thanks."

"That wasn't a compliment," he added.

I grinned as I kicked the bag hanging from the ceiling. I threw a few punches and stopped. I didn't need to train, all I needed was to get this far—closer to the exit. Turning to Lance, I tapped my finger on my chin.

"You know, I'm surprised Wes had just you guard me. He should know I can get past you if I wanted," I said.

He raised an eyebrow with his folded arms. "Is that so?"

I walked up to him. He looked worried but tried his best not to show it. He knew I would never physically hurt him, at least not outside of sparring—hence why he wouldn't fight me anymore. I placed my arms around his neck and smiled. "It is."

I kissed him, letting the narcotic on my lips to enter his mouth. He didn't resist. It was obvious he always wanted a kiss from me, though the only two times I had kissed him were for my own benefit, and ironically both on Valle. Realizing what I was really doing, he backed away, touching his lips and blinking. "Narcotics?"

I nodded. "Yup."

"Knew I wouldn't resist kissing you?" He leaned against the wall. It was already taking effect. I felt a little bad watching him as the drug worked its magic. He had been so nice, but hey, I didn't kill him like I could have.

"Yup."

He laughed. "Well played, Myra, well played."

Collapsing to the ground, I poked him with my foot. He would be out for a good hour or so. I turned back to the door and started towards the exit of the palace.

As I entered the corridors, I found the walls weren't lying. They warned me of another in the corridor, but I had hoped it was just a passerby. I was wrong. Wes was smart enough to have two guards watching me after the argument we had. Will, who was now lead general Alan Marc, stood in the corridor waiting for me. His dark hair was a contrast to his once blonde hair. His blue eyes pierced mine.

"So you were keeping watch as well," I said. "Should have known."

He stepped up to me. "We weren't stupid enough to let you just be alone with Lance, if you really wanted to get away from him it would be too easy."

I shrugged. "It was."

"Well, getting past me won't be."

"Really? I will be the judge of that."

He started to pull out his gun, but he was too slow. I shoved him against the wall. I heard the crackle of metal breaking from the wall behind me. His elemental power, unfortunately, was the ability to control metal. As I felt a sliver of metal enter my back, I kissed him as well. It really was the easiest way to knock him out, even though I would have to wash my mouth several times afterwards.

He jumped at the action, confused why I would kiss him, his eyes wide, but then he realized what was on my lips. He struggled for a second, but the narcotic took over fast. His body slumped to the floor.

I let it drop as I heard pieces of metal fall to the ground behind me. I turned, glad to have knocked him out before the bigger shards he pulled out of the wall got to me. I pulled out the small shard out of my back, grabbed his Class Two gun and kept on towards the exit. There was no one to stop me now. No regular human had a chance, nor would Wes think to send more backup. I had won this round.

Chapter 4

As I stepped outside, I took a deep breath of the fresh city air. Sure, it wasn't as refreshing as it was on Anosira, especially since there weren't that many more people on this planet compared to Anosira. I missed Anosira a lot, as I could have alone time, to walk outside and not see anyone for miles, to go out into the woods and peacefully sit and listen to the surrounding animals. But it was still nice not being locked away inside that building, but to walk freely without worry and with no one following me.

Well, that wasn't true. I hadn't detected them yet, so maybe I was wrong to think that the Pandronan Empire was keeping watch on us—that Neil still had an interest in me after all this time. He knew I would be the only one to find Sanshli again; he had to have known for a while without me ever suspecting. I was the daughter of Nygard, after all. What that meant, I still didn't have a clue. Most likely it just meant that being a monster was genetic.

Then there was my mother. The moment I passed a reflection of myself on a mirrored surface I would hear how wrong I was to run off like this—that it was a mistake and that I should turn back. I didn't care anymore; it was either this or kill my brother. I decided this was a little easier, and maybe I would find the one person who would make me smile again. That I would find Jack.

I missed Jack more than I thought I ever would. Sure, we spent a lot of time apart, but this was different. This time I didn't know where he was, I didn't know if he was okay or if he was even thrown into the past with us, though it seemed likely he found himself here. I wanted to go to Recar so many times, but my brother never allowed me. He made sure of that, especially since he had been spying for the Empire last time he saw him. It wasn't Jack's fault, though, Wes would have done the same if it were for Amanda.

My brother was blind with rage; I knew the feeling. When I was cooped up in the Kamps, all I wanted to do was kill the Emperor for hurting my family, for destroying the life I knew. But in fact, the Emperor had nothing to do with it. Garvner, in fact, was under attack because they had outright disobeyed the laws and comprised the P.A.E., Pirates Against Empire, sympathizers. It was them who cast down the fate of my

life; it was their fault for rebelling. I learned that from
Neil after he let me join his team. In the beginning, I used
my anger to fight, but Neil taught me so much more
about the galaxy and about life. Then I fought with a
clear head and I became a much greater fighter for it.

I just hoped I could control my powers soon, versus
only having the greatest strength when I was full of
emotional turmoil. I wanted to master them, be able to
do the same as Lance and the others, and be able to
control different elements. It wasn't fair that they could
train so easily over the past year and I could barely block
my mind from being read and intuitively be sense things
happening nearby. Strangely, no matter how hard I
concentrated, I couldn't figure out any of the other
powers of the Illusionist.

And yet, somehow, I had to find Sanshli and take
down one of the most powerful Illusionists in all of
history: my father. From what I gathered from my
mother, he was still on the planet, roaming around until
he could escape. I didn't understand why I couldn't just
leave him and call it good, but I guess then Neil or
someone like him could find the planet and he would
escape. Great. So I had to find the planet first, find the
book of spells, and somehow defeat him. Violet wouldn't
go into detail on how to do that. I was supposed "to
know when the time was right". Yeah, whatever that
meant.

I took a deep breath as I kept walking down the street.
It was strange, being able to walk around like this with
no one noticing me, or trying to ignore me. I was used to

worrying about people wanting to kill me, or people thinking I would kill them. Is this what being normal feels like? To not have to think about either of those things? To not be on a mission and to walk freely as everyone else did?

Unfortunately, I was on a mission, and there were a few enemies out there, who were observing me, waiting for the right moment when they thought I would let my guard down. They couldn't surprise me, though, they underestimated my instincts.

"What are you doing? I just told you not to leave." Mother finally came out of whatever place she had been to yell at me.

I sighed. *"I'm sick of waiting, I need to lead myself. I can't be under his thumb any longer."* I thought in my head. It wasn't like I could speak out loud without strangers looking at me like some kind of freak. Though I felt like one.

"You don't know what to do next, you aren't strong enough to face them."

"Then teach me!" I yelled inside my mind. *"All this time you have said that I need to learn, that I need to be protecting the universe, but all I have learned is blocking my mind! Illusionists are supposed to be able to do anything, but I have learned none of it."*

"But you haven't mastered blocking your mind, how can I teach you anything else if you can't even master that task?"

"I'm getting better at it, and besides, how am I supposed to know if I'm good at it if the people I am around aren't able to read my minds?" I asked.

"You need to be at full strength in order to be near those who can read your mind. If they can read your mind, we will lose everything and they will win."

"I am strong enough. Now, let me do this one on my own." I pushed her out of my mind. It took a lot of strength to accomplish, but it was possible. I got her to stop communicating with me.

I sighed. I felt alone in this world. Even with Violet talking to me, and always being there, it somehow made me feel even more lonely. It was a feeling I should have been used to, but it wasn't until now that I realized how important Jack had been in my life. Even though he didn't completely know me and we rarely got to see each other, he was still a figurative rope to grab while I was drowning.

Honestly, I never learned to trust anyone, even Jack. I learned to only trust my instinct of what I thought they would do. And I was very good at predicting things, other than this whole Sanshlian business. But for normal circumstances and missions, I was always one step ahead of everyone else. Though now with everything that had happened since finding Sanshli, it got a little harder.

But that didn't mean I was just going to stand around and wait for action to happen. I would make it come to me. That's what I was good at, which I wasn't sure was a good thing or a bad thing.

Neil always said that the way I fought, the way I could get under everyone's skin and piss them off was a good thing. I bet now he wasn't thinking that, though he was right, I was good at it. I just hoped there would be a way

I could get him to trust me again, to get him to believe that I wanted to help him. Really, I just needed help to find Sanshli so I could end this once and for all. And since Mother was teaching me how to pick what others could see in my mind, I could trick Neil.

I couldn't guarantee that Jack would be with them, or that in fact Neil or the other Generals were there. But it made sense that they would be, that those who fought for the Empire would appear on that side, as those who fought for the P.A.E. woke up on the Second Republic's side. Why I woke up with them, I did not understand.

It wasn't like I cared either way. My loyalty wasn't to the Second Republic for sure, and after everything, it wasn't for the Pandronan Empire neither. All I cared about at this point was going back home to the future, running away and never looking back. All I had to do was find the spell book and destroy Nygard's heart and then all would revert to normal. I wouldn't have to be the universe's only hope any longer and I could just disappear.

I was sick and tired of taking orders from people, I truly was. Between Neil, my brother, my mother, the Kamps' officers, I just wanted to be free. That was all I wanted for a while and I think after this was over, I would make it my reward. Freedom.

If I survived, that is.

Sure, it took a lot for me to be killed, as my brother figured out quickly, and I could heal fast. Even Lance and the others could heal faster than a normal human, and were a lot stronger with their new Sanshlian bodies, but I was still a lot stronger than them and could heal quite a bit faster. It must have been an Illusionist thing, not that I would know. My mother wouldn't teach me anything useful besides blocking my thoughts from being intruded upon.

And it wasn't like I would abuse that kind of power either, I didn't want it to take over the universe. I just wanted it so I could end this stupid legend. I just wanted to survive and live my life without this chafing sense of duty or destiny.

I kept walking forward, hoping that my brother hadn't noticed my absence yet and sent out a search for me. It wouldn't matter though, the people that have been following me for the past few blocks were about to attack. I ran through all the scenarios in my mind, wondering what would be the best way to let them capture me without raising suspicion. If it was who I thought it was, letting them capture me without a fight would let them know I wanted to be captured, and I couldn't allow that. So I would have to fight and slip up and lose. It would be painful, more so than what Alan had ever done to me.

An arm wrapped around me, forcing a cloth over my nose and mouth, but I was ready for him. I elbowed him in the stomach before the chloroform could enter my system. I would be damned before I would ever let someone get me with a cheap move like that. Not to mention it was weak and pathetic. Whoever was attacking me was not high up in the military world. That was such a rookie move.

I spun around and rammed my palm into the assailant's nose. Broke it the moment it was struck, letting me know they weren't Sanshlian for sure. The man hit the ground with a loud thud. I smiled triumphantly.

But that wasn't all of them. He was just the first.

Three other men surrounded me, their Class Three guns ready to shoot me down if I threatened them just like I did with the first. They wouldn't aim for a fatal shot, but would try to immobilize me. They could easily fix me up once I was taken, unfortunately. I didn't particularly want that to happen, I didn't want to gain more wounds to heal from, though I had the potential to heal from even the worst. Sure they weren't fatal, but damn did they hurt.

I pulled out my TG-2 and shot one of them while the other two tried to take me down. I moved out of the way quickly, their shots missing me by a hairsbreadth. It was too close for comfort.

Deciding that running away might be the best strategy in all of this, as I didn't want to feel the pain of a bullet, I bolted down the street, shoving people out of my way as the men followed close behind. They tried to hide their guns in the street, worried that law enforcers would see them. I didn't want to be caught by any either and tucked my gun back underneath my jacket.

I wasn't sure how many there were in the area, and I still wasn't even sure how big the Pandronan Empire was or how it even first formed or why. I had no idea how many men they would send after me, especially if someone from the past was in charge. I figured that they were probably thrown into the bodies of the Imperials, just as Rik had been for the Second Republic, but I didn't know that for a fact.

I didn't know Valle as well as I knew many other planets. It wasn't like I could venture around the city now or in the future when I was the Emperor's Shadow. Since they saw me as their enemy, traveling to Valle was never a wonderful idea, and Wes didn't let me out of his sight, so I never got out that often.

So I had no idea where I was going as I ran away from these men that shot at me. No officers seemed to patrol the area, helping keep the streets safe. They must have sent out a decoy, drawing the officers away from this area with a robbery or something so they didn't have to worry about being interrupted. They had this planned for a while now, and they were waiting for me.

I hurried around another corner to find it to be a dead end. *Shit*. I turned around to face my assailants. There were four of them, all in hooded jackets. Why did everyone think hoods helped? I didn't think so.

In each of their hands was a Class Three gun pointed at me. I debated whether it would be best to defend myself or just let them take me where they wanted me to go. But if I did that, they would know I was trying to be caught.

So I guess I would just do this the hard way.

Pulling out the Class Two gun I took from Alan, I shot the man on the left. The other three started for me, readying their own guns to fire. I ran forward before they could finish the shot and punched one of them out. I swept the legs out from underneath the other man. I had three down and one to go.

At least I had thought it was just one. Apparently I was wrong. There were more in the surrounding areas. Whoever was behind this made sure there were more than I could handle, if that was possible. If I wanted to get away, I could have the advantage over this fight, no matter the number.

I used the butt of the gun on the one left before thinking about dealing with the five more assailants that were now surrounding me. He went down as easily as his partners.

"I take it you are from the Pandronan Empire," I laughed. "You all need to brush up on your fighting skills if you want to win this war."

None of the men answered, but I knew they thought that if they failed, a worse fate was waiting for them. So they were fighting with all the strength they had. I had to give them respect—few would accept this mission. Then again, I doubt any of them volunteered for this.

I ran straight towards the group, the element of surprise on my side. They jumped out of the way as I pushed past, heading down the street once again. I heard them curse and yell to run after me once again. I was giving them a run for their money and damn did I miss that.

But of course, I turned down another dead end. How many dead ends were in this city anyway? It was like the city wanted me to be captured, to return once more to the Empire where my kind belonged. I wouldn't blame it, maybe it knew the fate I would bestow on it if I stayed. Maybe it knew about all the PAE agents I had killed over the years.

Damn, the planet was smarter than I gave it credit for.

As I turned around, I found five guns raised at me.

"Come with us and we won't have to shoot."

I laughed. "Would he let you damage his goods?" I asked as I stepped forward. One soldier shot me straight in the leg. I went down to my knees. "Damn it," I cursed.

"Move again and I will shoot again. Is that clear?" The man yelled down at me.

I sighed as I stood back up. "But staying still would be out of character for me." I pulled my gun up and was about to shoot back when I felt another bullet hit me in the shoulder. I dropped the gun as pain shot through my arm. I fell down, pain consuming my body. The bullets had to have been laced with something very potent, as I could feel my body weakening, becoming immobile.

"Were those..." I could barely talk, unconsciousness raining down upon me. "Laced?"

"As ordered," the soldier said as he knelt down beside me. "But just in case..." He placed a rag over my mouth and I couldn't help but breathe in.

A few moments later, everything went black.

Chapter 5

Icy floor. It had been a while since I had woken on a cold metal floor. My eyes flickered open to find myself where I expected to be: locked in a cell. Standing up, I rubbed my head. This body, although it could heal quite quickly, was still not quite used to narcotics like my last one had been. The ache went away though, and I felt my shoulders once again. My shirt and jacket were caked in blood, but there was no more pain. They must have taken the bullet out and left it alone. I checked my leg. Same thing, just blood but no more pain.

Which meant someone here knew exactly who I was. I had been right about Neil and the others all along. Now the question was, would this reunion be a good or bad one?

I looked around. The ship was definitely Imperial; I

recognized the cell as one of the old ships we still had on Anosira. It was still making my head spin at the thought of what was past and future anymore. I rubbed my head again. Although the narcotics had worn off, thinking about everything still made my head hurt. I still didn't know whose side I was on. I hated my brother; I hated everything he was doing. Nothing could change my mind about him and wanting to drive a sword through his heart. But the Emperor had been using me this entire time and just discarding me like a tool once I became useless. He was not any better.

But I was always his tool before that, wasn't I?

I always told myself I belonged to the Emperor and the Emperor alone. He could do whatever he wanted with me and I didn't care about repercussions. So why did I make such an enormous deal when the actual reason he wanted me was to find Sanshli? He didn't treat me any differently from he had before. I was just a means to an end, and if I was in the same position, would I not do the same? I would have, after all the missions I had been on and all the destruction I had caused for others. I had caused many people a lot of pain. So maybe I threw things out of proportion. Maybe I had been hanging around my brother too much. Or Jack.

I put my hand on my chest and took a deep breath. My heart felt as if it skipped a beat every time I thought of Jack. The pain wouldn't go away. The deep feelings I had for him I never realized were there until now. I didn't know where he was or where he could be. I wanted to search for him, but I had no idea where to even start. *Was he with the Emperor? Or was he back on Recar? If so, who would he be?* Sure, there were crime-lords semi-ruling Recar at the moment, but there were also representatives of the Second Republic and such. He could be anywhere.

And since my brother saw him as a traitor, I wasn't able to go looking for him. Not to mention if Wes found out my true feelings for him, he would use it against me. I was supposed to be the cold-hearted killer the entire universe saw me as being, I couldn't show love. I wasn't allowed to love, to understand what it meant to lose someone. No, I was just a heartless creature that causes destruction wherever she went. Never meant to have an actual life.

Placing my hand on the cool metal wall, I listened to the heart of the ship. Yes, we were in space; I could feel the humming of the engine. The people walking through the corridors. There weren't many of them. If I wanted to, I could take them all out. But I didn't want to. Not yet, anyways.

"Anybody interested in talking to me? Ask me some questions?" I shouted. There was no response. Usually someone would have been sent in by now, since I had just woken up. There were camera feeds in each cell. They would have known I was awake by now. They were just testing me. "If you wait long enough, maybe I will just bust out of here and find you myself!"

Nothing.

It could never be easy, could it? That I would wake up and the person who captured me would be waiting and then explain everything to me so I was up to speed. No, it was never like that. I always needed to make a big scene before I was told anything, kill a few people if I must. It was like the person who captured me wanted to test my patience.

And guess what? I had no patience.

I shrugged, laughing. It had been a while, having to act like my old self, both teasing and cocky, not letting anything take me down. I was impervious in this state of mind, I mean, other than doing stuff to Lance, but that was a little different, not to mention I still let up at times. Here I could finally give it all I got.

And it felt great.

Wes had made it so I had to hold back, knowing he would give Alan the order to kill me if I tried anything foolish. It was ridiculous, really, how he hid behind Alan and Lance from me. If it was a one-on-one fight, I would win in an instant. And he knew that.

So Neil was testing me, he had to have been, to see if I changed, to see if being with my brother all this time had weakened me somehow, or to see if I was still the fighter that I once was. The fighter that I will always be.

I couldn't let him down, now could I?

I wanted him to trust me again, to have him think I had seen the error in my ways, that I had been a fool this whole time and should have been serving him just as I had promised. It made me want to gag just thinking about it, but I had to keep up the farce. I had to make him think I still wanted to serve him.

So that meant I had to be the old me. I had to be cocky, heartless, and a ruthless killer. It would be easy because I hadn't changed all that much.

"All right then, I guess I will come find my captor *myself.*"

The camera, although invisible to the naked eye, was in the very center of the ceiling, which is rather hard to get to with no help. But when you were an assassin, or the Shadow of the Emperor, you could get to it. I jumped off the side of the cell and up to where the camera would be. I was able to break the lens on my first try. Normally a human wouldn't have that ability, but I wasn't human. I was a Sanshlian that also had inhuman strength.

Now I needed to find a way out of here before they came to teach me a lesson about breaking expensive equipment. How did I know it's expensive? Well, because this wasn't my first time breaking one. And I learned my lesson about breaking expensive equipment.

There was a vent on the ceiling. There was always a vent on the ceiling. Trick was knowing which panel was where that vent lay hidden. They all looked the same, but when you had been captured as many times as I had, you know which one it is. Jumping up, I punched the crate open. It made a loud crash and still no one came to see what the noise was.

I concluded that they wanted me to escape. Whoever was behind all of this was waiting for me somewhere. *Was I that predictable?* They should know better than this, letting me be able to move with no kind of hindrance. Climbing up into the shaft, I ventured towards a different part of the ship.

I could feel the ship moving, breathing as if it were

alive. It was a strange sensation that I had now, being able to hear and feel things that others could not. Sure, I used to have dreams and be able to heal quite quickly, but this was different. This was more intimate. And it wasn't just with ships, but any building, any forest, any place. It felt as if it were alive, and I could hear it.

Although I was never truly alone with Wes always checking on my whereabouts, I always considered myself to be alone. With these new powers, for once in my life I felt connected to something, that I wasn't merely just a lost girl trying to find her way through the universe. I had Jack, yes, but at the moment I had no idea if he was here, or even alive.

I pushed the thoughts of Jack to the back of my mind. I didn't want to think of him in a time like this, when I need to concentrate on the task at hand, which was impressing Neil. He was the only one who could be behind this as he would be the only one searching for me, other than Wes. But if it were Wes, Alan would have already come to knock me around some, maybe even get in a shot or two for knocking him out like I had.

No, this had to be Neil. It felt like him. That, and I didn't sense any presence I was familiar with in this timeline. I didn't know if I could sense people from the future in their new bodies, as I had only been around David and the others.

And how did they know where I was? It wasn't like Wes ever let me out of his sight, or out in the open. No one except those close to the Republic knew I existed. The outside world was oblivious. So whoever it was had to be from the future.

And if it was, I would be one step closer in finding a way home.

Home. I almost let out a laugh. I never thought I considered a place to be my home. Even on Garvner, I didn't feel at home and finding out that I was from Sanshli made me understand I had been from another life, living in one that shouldn't have been mine. I wondered how they tricked Father into adopting me, and why he never said anything about it. It was because he would wait until I was older, at an age where I could understand. I missed him and loved him more knowing that he treated me like his own daughter when I was in fact not. If, in some strange circumstance, I was able to see him again, I would thank him for everything.

It was also strange because I had seen photos of when I was just a baby. But from what I knew, Myra, as in myself, was a little girl of about three or four when she was hidden from Nygard. I did not understand how that was possible or what had happened.

I wished Father had never been shot, that he never had to get in the middle of all of this. This whole time he was trying to help my mother in destroying Nygard. This whole time he knew the truth, knew I wasn't his daughter, and he never told me. But that was why he had the keys and the pocket watch that were still snug in my pocket. It was all to fulfill the prophecy. He gave his life so I could go on, so that the universe could be saved somehow, but not by doing my brother's or Neil's bidding. I had to be a rogue agent.

I would finish that conquest, if not for the Sanshlians, but for Father's sake. I wouldn't let him die for nothing. I couldn't, not after everything he had given me, and everything he wanted to give me.

As I put my hand forward on the vent shaft, I heard a creak and the panel under me shudder.

"Ah, shit," I whispered as the entire panel fell down and I with it. I slammed into a metal table, bruising even more bones from the impact.

Good thing I could heal fast, otherwise that would have ended a lot worse, and a lot more embarrassing.

"Ow..." I rolled over to find a man sitting at the desk. His blue eyes watched me as I stared at him. Although they were light, something inside of his eyes were dark, I could tell. He was not a person to be reckoned with, that I knew for a fact. He wore a suit and had short black hair with a trimmed beard to match.

"Nice of you to drop by." The man grinned, though it was fake. He appeared as if he was hiding something, as if the smile on his lips was just a mask, something he had mastered to hide his true feelings. And what those were, I wasn't sure.

"So I was correct, you expected me to escape," I said as I sat up, my body shooting out signals of something having been fractured. It was going to take a few hours to get that to heal. How I could be so unlucky, I had no idea. I swore when Violet sent me to the future, she also cast out a curse on me, one that made my life full of pain. Or maybe it was Nygard, I couldn't be sure.

The man shrugged. "I wouldn't expect anything less

from you."

I glanced around the room. It was a standard interrogation room, one I found myself on the other side of the table of. Usually I was the one asking questions, more through use of actions rather than words though. And by actions, I meant punching, stabbing, and kicking until grown men wept for their mothers and told me everything I needed to know.

And as with any other interrogation room, there was a mirrored wall. One which held a reflection of my mother staring right back at me. Could my interrogator see this reflection, or could only I see it?

"Shield your mind," she ordered.

"Why?"

"Because you don't know who he is." With that, she disappeared.

I took a deep breath and shielded the thoughts I didn't want this man to see, if he even could. I agreed that I should have been doing that already, but being away from my brother left me curious and I almost felt free, so I forgot about the minor things. From now on, I would keep my mind shielded, just as she wanted.

I turned back to my interrogator and grinned. "So, who do you work for?"

The man just laughed and scratched his scruffy beard. "You are a very interesting character, Arcadia. Always asking the questions even when you are on the opposite side of the table. Even when you are the one who should be answering the questions."

"Heh, that's for sure. But you know who I am, so I am

at a disadvantage." Because I had no idea who he was, other than he was obviously from the future, or at least was told of my existence.

"Of course I do, you worked under me most of your life. I just can't believe you don't recognize your master when he sits in front of you."

I stared at him for a second longer, then jumped to my feet. I should have recognized him, the first emperor of the Pandronan Empire all those years ago. I had been taught all about the history of the Empire, seen so many pictures, so many videos of the war by Neil. Yet I didn't even recognize him as he sat in front of me.

Not only that, but it also meant he could only be one person from the future. The one person I had been looking for, the one person who I had hoped was looking for me.

"Neil."

Chapter 6

"Sir," I knelt down on my knees, grimacing in pain as my leg that had been fractured from the fall. I would take the pain, though, because I knew he could and would cause worse if he thought it necessary.

The Emperor stood up, circling me as if he was examining his prey. "I find it interesting that you bow to me. After all, last time we saw each other you wanted to kill me."

"That seems like a lifetime ago," I stated, although in a way it was a different lifetime. Time travel really put things in perspective, not to mention it has given me many headaches trying to fathom all the paradoxes and implications, "And I realized I was wrong to hate you. You were the one that trained me, I should have followed your orders. I should have destroyed the enemy when ordered. I deserve any punishment you give to me. My life is in your hands as it always has been and always will be."

Neil laughed. "Words I thought I would never hear you say." He looked at me for a moment, probably reading my mind as he apparently did whenever we were together. It was strange to think he knew all the things I was thinking over the years. Then again, it explains why every time I tried to kill him, he was always one step ahead of me.

His eyes softened after he read the lies that filled my head. "And you are telling the truth. You regret turning against me."

Good thing Violet taught me how to shield my mind, and to fabricate false thoughts for those who could read minds. She knew that one day this would come to pass, that my enemy were those who could read minds. Strange to think his family were one of the ones who had served under Nygard, that they had been searching for the planet and statue for all these years.

"Please take me back to serve you. I regret ever letting anything come in the way of my duties. I was confused, everything was new to me, overwhelming. I panicked when I should have remained loyal."

He examined me closely, as if not believing in what I was saying. "Even after using you? Even after leaving you there to die? Letting you go insane from all the voices of the ghosts that remain trapped there?"

"You had to do what you needed to do. I betrayed you, I deserved it," I repeated. It was true, I deserved any punishment for all the things I had done in my life. I deserved to be killed for all the things I did under his order. It didn't mean I still hated him for using me all those years, him never telling me the truth about my past. I didn't let those thoughts show in my mind.

He placed his finger underneath my chin and lifted it to make me look at him. Now I recognized those deceiving eyes. They were the same as the ones his original body had. It made sense, seeing as how this man would be his many-greats grandfather. "So the voices are gone?"

I nodded. It had been such a long time I had forgotten about them. "They are."

"Before or after we came here?"

"A moment before."

He smiled. "So you solved it? Just before it happened."

I raised my eyebrow. How did he know so much about Sanshli and I knew nothing? "Solved what?"

"What happened after you pulled out the sword."

"I did, and I tried to stop my idiot brother but it was too late. He let his feelings impede his thinking and didn't stop when I yelled for him to. Now here we are."

Neil nodded, examining me as if I was spectacular to watch. "I'm impressed, Arcadia, no one has ever solved the problem of how to get those voices out of their head. I have heard of so many people before you killing themselves, seeing no escape, yet you got them to go away in mere minutes."

"Yeah, well, I'm special like that." I tried to act like it was no big deal, but just thinking about those voices, how loud they were, how much they took over my mind, I shuddered. If I had had to endure them any longer, I probably would have been one of the many who put a bullet in their head.

"So you are." He tapped the table, as if thinking it all through. "Question is what should I do with you?"

So he still wasn't sure. That was positive on my end because then I could get him to believe that I wanted to help, that I would be a great aid for his cause. I could hide the fact that I wanted to punch him in the nose, let it heal, then do it again, till I felt vindicated for all he'd put me through.

But I wouldn't let him know that. "Please, sir, I will do anything for you. I will never go against anything you say. I will do anything you want me to do, just let me serve you." I put my head down, staring at the floor, surrendering myself to him. I had to make it look genuine. "I am begging you, sir, please."

He laughed at me, seeing me in such a state. I wish I didn't have to do this, I hated looking like a weakling. "Is your brother really that horrible to deal with that you would bow down to me once again?"

I looked back up at him, trying to hide my amusement at his dead-pan comment. "He's a traitor to anything sacred. He is committing genocide. His next attack is on Ttkas, I can give you all the details I have learned."

A sliver of a smile appeared on his lips. "I believe you have destroyed quite a number of people yourself. You are anything but innocent, Arcadia, or I should say Myra. What *do* you go by now?"

"Those people committed crimes against the Empire's law. The people Wes is destroying are innocent people. He is destroying people before they have done anything. I can't allow that," I explained. "And I go by Myra. It is my original name, and the name of this body."

"Strange being in another's body, isn't it?" he asked.

I nodded. "It is, but I have gotten used to it. After the past year, I have been able to get my muscles and muscle memory to do what it once was trained to do. It took a while, but I am as strong as I was before."

"Not stronger?" he asked.

I tried not to let out a sigh, but failed. "I... haven't been able to master my powers. I don't know how to learn to be an Illusionist. I can heal for sure, but I can't do anything else."

"What about the others? Your brother and his friends?"

"They each have unique powers but even with them I could defeat them with no problem. I got away, didn't I?"

Neil stepped around the table and looked at the mirror. I stayed still, my leg throbbing in pain. I wondered what he was thinking, if he was still trying to read my mind. I can't even imagine all the thoughts he had read over the years. He knew everything about me and I knew nothing about him, at least not truly. I knew that his parents had been assassinated when he was young, that he was born to his position. Now I knew he was a Sanshlian as well and could read minds, born in a lineage that served Nygard and would do anything to bring their master back. Other than that, I didn't know much about him.

He turned back to me. "So if I ordered you to, you would kill your brother?"

I let out a sharp laugh. "I have tried to kill him already. Problem is, there is always someone to stop me before I succeed."

"That has never stopped you before." He paused, letting the information linger in his mind. "Which means there is someone there you don't want to kill."

That was true. I could never let Lance come to harm, maybe deep down I cared for him. That was probably the real reason I never killed my brother. That and I imagined our father haunting us until the end of time. "If you gave me the orders, I would kill any of them, sir."

"No, I think there is one whom you will not kill. David, or I guess Lance now. Your mind betrays you, Myra. You know you can't hide anything from me."

I wanted to slap myself across the face for letting that information slip into my mind at just the wrong moment. I should have been more careful. But it took me by surprise. I couldn't help but think of Lance when he brought up the face of someone I didn't want to kill, which showed I wasn't completely emotionally repressed. "He was the only who showed me compassion, yes, but my loyalty to you is greater. I will kill him if you want me to, you know that."

He scratched his chin, as if thinking what he should do with me. He captured me, though, did he not know what to do with me or was he just playing? "What would Jack say about your feelings for this man?"

My heart jumped at the name. "Is he with you?"

Smiling, Neil sat back down in the chair. I should have not been so fast to respond, I knew, but I had been wondering about his whereabouts for quite some time. I wanted to know if he was all right.

"That is the exact response I thought you would give me," Neil said. "You love him, don't you?"

I could feel my heart pounding in my chest. Even if I could block my thoughts out about Jack, there was no way he would believe them. He knew my genuine feelings this entire time, he knew how much I cared about him before being separated from me. I couldn't lie, so I nodded. "I... I do."

"Exactly what I was afraid of." He let out a sigh, as if this wasn't something he wanted to deal with. I was just supposed to be his obedient servant, not with any emotions or strings attached. I messed that up by falling in love with the man I was supposed to kill all those years ago. Though if he thought it to be a problem, he should have had me kill him before those emotions developed to this point. Unless he was afraid I would run if I did that, and then his plan to use me to find Sanshli would be destroyed. But that was now over with, so what would he make me do?

"When we were transported into the past, he ended up with us," he explained. "On the Imperial side of the war."

I couldn't believe what I was hearing. Did I finally find him, after all this time? Could I know that he was okay, that he had survived traveling through time?

"So he is here?" I asked. I probably shouldn't have showed so much excitement, not when I was trying to prove my loyalty to him and him alone. This showed that there was someone else I cared for, someone else that could impede that loyalty.

"Yes, but Myra, might I add, if you want to serve me once again, you are not allowed to love him. You are not allowed to show him any kind of emotion. And more importantly, you aren't allowed to tell him why. He will try to talk you out of it, he will try to take you away. If I catch a hint of something going on, which I can because I can read both of your minds, I will dispose of him and I will make you suffer the consequences."

I watched Neil's leery eyes. He was serious. There would be no wiggle room with this. If I screwed up, Jack was a goner. There would be no way I would get Neil to trust me again, and it would shatter my heart. Not to mention it would ruin everything I needed to get us back to the future. I needed everyone there, and I didn't know what would happen if someone died. I didn't let Neil see that in my mind though. So I would go along with his stupid game. I would appease him and finally be free.

I nodded, reluctantly. "I understand."

He grinned, as if he had waited so long to hear me say that. "Good. He has been asking about you, knowing that we would capture you. He wants to see you again..."

"I will not show him any emotion. I will tell him... that I don't care for him anymore, not after everything that has happened. Not after how he betrayed me."

It would hurt, I knew, but it had to be done, at least until I sorted everything out and I took down Nygard and the Empire. Then I could tell him the truth, then I could be with him. I just had to wait a bit, but knowing he was alive and having him close by, I knew would be enough. At least that is what I hoped would prove satisfactory. But emotions of the heart are a fickle thing.

"Fine then." He stepped towards me, so that his legs were just inches from my feet. I looked up at him, still bowing down. My leg throbbed with pain still but it was dulling. "I will let you serve me again. Under supervision, of course."

"Oh, goodie, I get to be watched night and day again," I commented. All I needed was to be supervised again. It made me feel like a child, though even as a child I had more freedom than my brother gave or Neil would give me.

"There's my girl, attitude and all. I was wondering."

"You know me, I never change."

"Well, that isn't entirely true, but that's neither here nor there. All that matters now is that you keep up your training and serve me and me alone. Do you understand that?"

I nodded. "Yes sir."

"Good, then you should get to it." He started to leave the room. I knew he still didn't trust me, that this was a test, and he was monitoring my thoughts every moment he could. I couldn't slip up, but there was one thing I had to know.

"So you have known all along?" I asked as I stood up. I wanted to know, whether he had been reading my mind every second in the past, or if it was just certain times that where he focused and gleaned what he needed... If he had been reading my mind at any point, then he would have known about Father, my past, and everything Jack and I had done together, not to mention all the trouble I had gotten into on each planet, although that was all done under his orders.

He stopped and turned back to me. "That my girl has been going behind my back and shacking up with a crime-lord? Yes, I have. It took everything for me not to kill him, but I couldn't because I had no proof. You hide your tracks well."

"That's because you trained me, sir."

He stepped up to me and slapped me across the face. "I trained you never to hide anything and to never go behind my back, is that clear?" His voice was harsh, dark, and I didn't want to imagine what he would do to me if I ever betrayed him again.

I nodded. "Yes, sir."

"Now, it will be awhile before we reach Anosira. Go meet with Dan. He will be your trainer from here on out."

"Of course," I said. He turned and walked out of the room. I took a deep breath, letting the pain escape my chest. It would take a while to get used to shrugging Jack off, as he was persistent, which was how I got in this mess the first time. I didn't want either of us to get hurt, though it was better than getting killed, as I had seen the anger in Neil's eyes. No, I wouldn't allow anything to happen to Jack and I could explain everything after this journey was over.

Chapter 7

As ordered, I hurried into the training room to find this 'Dan' that Neil had ordered me to work with. I wondered what could be so special about him to have Neil want him to train me. I had been training on my own for so long, I didn't understand what else I could be taught. Curiosity piqued my interest, curiosity of what kind of person could be stronger and better at fighting than me.

The training room was empty, as usual. Soldiers and guards seemed to get lazy on ships, or they just enjoyed staying away from me. Usually it was the latter, especially on a Representative's ship. Aboard ships, people seemed to fear me all the more. I never quite understood why, if I wanted to hurt or kill them, I wouldn't have gone to the trouble of traveling with them. It would be unnecessary.

However, these men didn't know that about me, and how could they? They weren't used to me, they didn't fear what I could do to them. Hadn't seen what I could do to a person in a single second. Not yet, anyway.

My leg was already feeling better. That was one great thing about being an Illusionist. I didn't have to worry so much about my injuries, as they quickly healed themselves. I was still covered in blood, but I didn't care. I could just clean up after training.

Starting my normal routine, I stretched for a bit and then slammed my fist again and again into the bag of sand that hung from the ceiling. I had no idea where Dan was or what he even looked like, so I took the opportunity of being alone and use it to my advantage. It had been a while since I could do this alone and it felt good to get my frustrations out. Usually Lance was with me, talking my ear off as I tried to concentrate. He was the only one who wasn't afraid to annoy me all this time, though I had been close to punching him in the mouth many times, hoping that would stop him from talking. I never did though, I was too nice with him.

I kicked the bag again. Why I kept thinking about Lance, I wasn't sure. Did I care for him like Neil thought I did? Or was it just that I wasn't used to someone wanting to spend time with me, other than Jack. Did I see him as a replacement for Jack and that was all? And when I found Jack, would I just toss Lance out like he was just trash? No, even though many thought I was heartless, I wasn't that bad. I had promised Neil that if need be, I would kill Lance for him. That was a lie conjured up for Neil to see as truth when reading my thoughts. I just hoped it wouldn't come to where I needed to choose.

How many lives of those I loved would I watch be destroyed before this was all said and done?

The Empire had taken everything from me. Father. My childhood. Happiness. Loyalty. Sanity. Now my love. Neil had taken Jack away from me, and with that he had everything at this point. I was just a puppet, one that was made only to serve him. I knew it would happen, eventually, when he figured it out. *At least he isn't dead*, I told myself, *at least I could still see him regularly. At least I didn't have to kill him myself.*

I jumped up and round-house kicked the bag. It felt good to have some peace, to be away from David, from my brother, and all of the Republic. Yes, I was still under close watch, but I felt a little freer here, like I belonged, even though I had everything taken away from me by this Empire, both past and future.

Maybe that was why I felt free. I had nothing.

I shook off these thoughts. I didn't like where I was, honestly never did. It was that or death. Neil had taken me from the Kamps and I was thankful for that. I was thankful that I didn't die that day when I tried to kill him. I punched the bag again. It was all messed up, I didn't know what to think anymore. I just knew I needed to take Nygard down so we could return to the future. So we could all live our lives at last.

"You need better form," I heard a voice say behind me.

I whipped around, curious who was standing behind me. I didn't hear anyone come in. Was that because he was very good at sneaking around or because I had been so focused on punching the bag? Either way I should have been more alert and if Neil was around, I would have been reprimanded.

"Hi," he said. The man was taller, with reddish-blonde hair. His eyes were a bright blue as they glistened with his smile. He wore a black shirt with baggy pants to match. I felt as if I had seen him before, but no idea where.

"Hi," I repeated, confused why such a simpleton would ever comment on my form.

He looked me up and down, as if the sight of all the blood confused him, but he didn't say a word. He stretched out his hand. "I'm Dan. Joss sent me to monitor you."

"Joss? Oh right," I said, ignoring the gesture of the handshake. Joss was Neil's new name, or old name I guess. Stupid time travel things confusing my poor little brain. Either way, it was his name now, and I needed to get used to that. "He sent you?"

He took his hand back. "Yeah, and by the looks of it I can see why. I will help you train."

I turned back to the bag. "I don't need any help."

Dan laughed. "Yes, you do, your form is all wrong."

I turned back to him, a little pissed, wondering if Joss sent him because he wanted to make me angry. He enjoyed doing that sometimes. "Excuse me? I have been doing this for years. I'm trained in ways that would baffle your mind."

"Really?" He examined me for another second. He seemed confused, and I wanted to smack that look right off his face. "Doesn't show."

I took a deep breath, trying not to let my anger get the better of me. I didn't need this pip-squeak telling me in what ways I was weak. He may have been older than me by a good number of years, but that didn't mean he knew more than me. That didn't mean he had lived through the things I had lived through. "I'm not a person you want to irritate, I don't want to get in trouble with Joss for beating you into a pulp on the first day, though I'm sure he wouldn't be surprised."

The threat didn't seem to make him waver. "Try me."

"Excuse me?" I couldn't believe what I was hearing. No one wanted to duel with me, except Lance sometimes, but he was an exception. And I was always easy on him. Really easy.

He raised his hands up, his palms opened instead of closed into fists. Few people used that as their defense, so I had to give him some credit. He had some background in fighting.

"Try to beat me. That's an order as your trainer."

I shook my head. This man was a lunatic, thinking he could beat me. "Do you have a death wish?"

"Yes."

He threw a punch, but I blocked. I tried to punch back, but he blocked it. He was strong for his physique. He kept a smile the entire time he blocked all my punches.

"Come on, Myra, I thought you said I was no match

for you. Prove to me you are as strong as you say you are."

Trying to keep calm and not let my anger get the better of me, as anger always clouded my judgment, I tried to sweep underneath his legs but he was ready for that. He countered my attack, leaving me to fall to the ground. I stared up at him. I couldn't believe it. No one had ever made me fall before, not unless I dragged them down with me, which is how Tom and I ended up. I swore he always did that on purpose and liked it when I pulled him down with me. Damn, he was such an ass.

Walking over to me, Dan let out his arm to help me up. I grabbed it and let him help me up. At least he was a gentleman about it, at least he didn't rub it in my face that I had lost after boasting about how powerful I was. Instead, he had that soft smile on his face.

"Again," he said.

To say I was frustrated was an understatement. No one had defeated me in all these years, and I didn't want to admit defeat. Instead I raised my hands, ready to fight again. I wouldn't let him get the better of me again, I would not let him knock me down. I had been taken by surprise the first time, it wouldn't happen again.

It wasn't just luck on this man's side; he was better than me, and he wanted to prove it. So he knocked me down again and again. I wanted to kill him, yet was intrigued that he could take me down so easily. He knew fighting skills that I had never seen before, and I had been trained by fighters all throughout the universe. It must have been some lost art that had disappeared with the collapse of the Republic. I knew near the end of this that I had to have him train me.

The worse part of it all was the fact the smile on his face never left. He thought this was fun. He enjoyed fighting. It wasn't a smile for proving me wrong, but more of a comforting smile, one trying to show me what I could be capable of if I let him teach me. And after hitting the ground for the fifth time, I knew I had to let him teach me.

He said his name was Dan. I didn't remember a man named Dan in the history books. He must have been insignificant, just a soldier of some sorts. His face seemed similar, like someone I had met before and killed so many people in my lifetime that he could just have looked like someone else. I had noticed that through the years, that so many people had a lot of similar qualities. It was interesting. But the way he acted, the way he fought, there was no way I had ever met him before, I would have remembered.

Because that would have meant I failed at defeating him, and I never failed at defeating anyone, including Thomas, although Thomas would disagree. Jack had beaten me a couple of times, though, but not very fairly, so they didn't count.

The first time I met Jack, he won against me. It was my first real mission and although I had failed in my orders to kill Jack, Neil decided it would be best to write up a treaty with him. This was half due to realizing that Jack would make a formidable ally, and half due to Jack threatening to kill me if he didn't comply. I doubt Jack would have actually killed me—he had taken a significant interest in me. Since then, when the two of us dueled, we were usually an equal match.

But this man named Dan was far from a fair match.

I wondered if it was this body I now possessed, as it wasn't the one I had when I served the Empire, or having been training with the Republic for a year that I had lost my strength and resolve, but I knew that wasn't the case. I could beat anyone I faced while training there, even Alan. Although I didn't know if Alan was that good or if his anger for me made it easier for me to win. He couldn't stand it when I defeated him, so I could focus better and win the match. So if it wasn't me, that just meant this guy was just fantastic.

Dan slammed me down on the ground again, my back glad I had something padded to land on. I let out a sharp laugh. Yes, I was frustrated at first, but now I just couldn't believe I had lost so many times in a row. After so many years of training, so many years of winning, I had found my match. It was remarkable. And I knew he would train me so that someday I could defeat him, and I would be the very best.

"No one has ever beat me," I said as he pulled me back up. He didn't even look as if he had broken a sweat. Whatever his training style was, I was ready to learn.

"Well apparently, no one knows how to fight," he mumbled more to himself than to me. He seemed a little disappointed that I had lost, which I wasn't sure why that was the case. Usually when I won, I was more content than worried about the person I was fighting.

"We should call it a day. Shall I show you to your quarters so you can wash up?"

So I wasn't going back to the cell. That was a good sign that Neil, or I guess Joss, has started trusting me again. That, or he knew I wouldn't risk taking over the ship. I had no reason. I hated my brother, and I would never go back there. And besides, I wanted to see Jack, even if I could never be with him. At least, not until this was over.

But that didn't mean I didn't have my own agenda. I would have to wait though, it would be a long time before I could do anything to finish finding Sanshli.

"Okay. But tomorrow you are training me," I said as I stretched out my arms.

Dan let out a brief laugh. "That sounded like an order. I didn't know you outranked me. In fact, I'm pretty sure I outrank you."

"Then I will tell Joss to order you to train me. He always wants me to be the strongest, with no weaknesses whatsoever. Looks like you are the only one who can achieve that goal."

"Well that's true. Then your training has already begun."

"Good, I wouldn't expect anything less."

"You are definitely everything I imagined you to be." He turned and led me out of the training room. I watched him closely, not quite sure what he meant by that. Did Joss tell him about me? Why? Maybe it was just to inform him how I acted, how I was to train with him. That would make sense, but I still wasn't sure. I felt as if something more was going on, and I had to figure out what that was.

Dan took me towards my quarters. Strangely enough, even though I knew he was hiding information, something about him made me trust him. I didn't know what it was, but I felt as if I knew him. He couldn't be Jack or any of the generals, I knew each of their fighting styles. No, this was someone from this time. But something about him was familiar.

We arrived at the quarters assigned to me. "Well, here it is. If you need anything, I will be in the lounge."

"You aren't going to stay and guard me?"

He gave me a puzzled look. "No, why would I do that?"

I shrugged. "I don't know, just used to it I guess."

"Don't worry, Myra, out of anyone in the galaxy, I trust you won't do anything stupid." With that, he left me standing there. I never had someone say that to me, not even Jack. He had just met me, and yet he trusted me. This day was becoming stranger and stranger.

I entered my quarters and turned on the shower. I waited for the water to warm up so I could let it wash away the crusted blood and sweat. I pulled off my clothes. I would definitely need fresh ones, but I had a feeling Joss already provided them in the dresser. He was always prepared like that.

Pulling out my pocket watch, I was glad that I grabbed it before I left. It was my only connection to my past, to a much simpler time than now. I enjoyed having it tucked away in my pillow on nights that I couldn't sleep, listening to the predictable ticking as time went on, almost taking me back to somewhere I could be happy. I placed it on the table.

"*Is this where you really want to be right now?*" Violet questioned in the bathroom mirror.

"Better than with Wes," I answered.

"*You think you can handle them already?*" Her eyes looked worried.

I sighed as I turned to face her. "You have taught me everything you said you would teach me. I figured it was as good a time as any to come here."

"*Now you know what you need to do.*"

I nodded. "I know. Find the clue, solve it, find Sanshli and destroy Nygard once and for all."

Chapter 8

The next day, as Dan promised, we began our training. Before I met with him, I felt excited, which was strange since I hadn't felt this sensation in quite some time. I could barely sit still during breakfast, wanting to pace back and forth as I waited for him to come retrieve me. After about an hour of waiting, he appeared, looking as content as he did the day before. I didn't know how he could do it, how he could serve Joss with such a smile. Was Joss nicer now in the past than he was in the future? Or was he just nicer to Dan than he had ever been with me?

Dan took me to the training room where we began with some stretching and meditation. I had tried meditation before, and found that it worked for my mind, but hardly used it. It took time, and I didn't feel as if I was getting stronger, although it helped me find a little peace of mind when I was with Wes. However, I couldn't relax any of these times as I felt Lance was always staring at me. He thought I didn't notice, but I did. I knew he used that time to watch me closely, and dream about the things he wanted to do with me. And that was just what they were: dreams.

After meditation, he started teaching me his ways of fighting. I was lucky I could heal so fast as he dislocated my shoulder a couple of times as he flung me over his back. He was worried that he had hurt me, which he had, but I shrugged it off as I always did. No pain, no gain, right?

There were no other generals on the ship which I was rather happy about. I didn't want to deal with Thomas, Laura, or Peter at the moment, especially Thomas, as I was trying to concentrate on my training. They always got in the way, and Tom would just want to prove himself, and I didn't want to deal with that again. It would just make him madder at me and he would think he would have to be more of an ass towards me. It was a never-ending cycle with him.

Not to mention Tom knew that I was a Kamps child now. Then again, the reason I was made into the Emperor's Shadow was because I was a Sanshlian. It had nothing to do with my strength or Neil wanting to save me from the fate of death. All he wanted was to bring Nygard back to rule, as he was his servant, being a Sanshlian as well.

I couldn't believe that this entire time Neil had been a

Sanshlian, that all the Emperors were descendants of the Sanshlian race, that they were searching for Sanshli so that they could bring their beloved master back. And they had even found the planet before, Brayen, the guardian of Sanshli, taking care of them, or going insane by touching the doorknob of where Nygard was being held. I knew what that was like; I knew how easy it would have been for them to go insane.

As I fought against Dan, he tried to do one of his techniques, but I blocked him. I grinned. I was one step closer at getting stronger than him.

"Marvelous job. Now block this." He countered my punch and seconds later I ended up on the ground. I sighed as he helped me up.

"Again?" I asked.

He nodded. "Until you can beat me, your training will never be over."

"Sounds fair." I raised my hands in defense, but it was no use. No matter what type of style I used against him, he could take me down in an instant.

"You need to keep your guard up. You promise you had training experience?" he asked.

I gave him a look. "Yes. I have been training all my life, ever since…" I stopped, not wanting to go into the details of my kidnapping. I wanted to forget about the Kamps, forget about everything that had happened before. I just wanted to make everything right again, although I knew that was near impossible to achieve.

"What happened?" Dan asked as he sat down. "If you want to tell someone about it, I am all ears."

I stared at him for a moment, wondering why he was so nice to me in this way. It felt nice, yes, but I couldn't help but be suspicious. No one had ever cared, other than Jack. And he just wanted to get on my good side so I would come back more. Well, that wasn't true. I didn't doubt Jack's love for me, but in the beginning I was just a fascination to him, nothing more. This guy just wanted to know more about me. As if he truly cared.

I shrugged it off. "Doesn't matter. What matters is becoming stronger, being able to defeat anything that comes in my path."

"Is that the way you want to run away from your past?"

I narrowed my eyes. "Why do you care? It's none of your business."

"I think if you open up more, you could have a better time learning your strengths. Having just a hard heart will get you nowhere. Believe me."

For a moment, I saw something in his eyes. They were no longer cheerful, but dark and miserable, as if he had to face something in his past just as I had. Maybe that was why he wanted to know, because he understood.

But I didn't care. My past was my business, not his. I wouldn't tell some stranger about it, not after so many people had betrayed me in my past. I didn't feel I could trust him, but something deep down inside of me wanted to open up to him. I wouldn't let it take over my common sense, though, but I also wanted to know why that part of me wanted to believe in him.

"I know my past makes me who I am, what makes me

strong. But I don't need to tell some stranger about it. I just need you to make me stronger."

He studied me for a moment longer, then smiled. "If that is your wish, then that is what you will receive." He held up his hand. "Help me up?"

I grabbed his hand, and he pulled me down to the ground as he got up. "Biggest thing you need to learn, trust no one else."

That was surprising to hear him say, especially when he wanted me to open up to him, unless that was part of the lesson, to see if I would trust him. Well, I wouldn't, and especially not now. He made that clear.

Training went on for another few hours when we took a break and had something to eat. The food on the ship, as normal, was crap. I couldn't wait until we got to Anosira where the food would have some taste and variety even. But at least it was something, and not David trying to cook. If he could figure a way to do it, he could burn cereal.

I just grabbed a sandwich, egg salad, which probably isn't the safest choice but it looked the most appetizing. I then sat down at an empty table. Dan soon joined me.

"Enjoying yourself so far?" he asked as he took a bite of his sandwich.

I gave him a look. "Yes, I love getting slammed down repeatedly by a pipsqueak like you."

He laughed. "You definitely have a tongue on you. That's exactly what Joss warned me about. He said it surprised even him sometimes, after all the times you have been punched or slapped for talking back."

"Yeah, well I was never good at learning those lessons, especially since all those who have hurt me for it are dead now. Except Joss, that is." I took a bite of my sandwich. Yup, it was horrible, just as I thought. "How did you get to be working with Joss? Why did you choose the Empire?"

"I always liked the idea of an Empire, as long as it's controlled by the right person. So much good can be done with that kind of power," he explained. I was surprised by his answer, as he seemed like a pleasant guy. Few kind people liked an Empire, especially since it could be easily corrupted. Then again, Wes had corrupted the Second Republic pretty easily as well. Maybe there was no suitable way to rule a galaxy. It all just had to do with the people behind it. The system was broken unless altruistic people ruled.

"And you think Joss is the right person?" I asked, because I sure as hell didn't. Though it was a toss-up between him and Wes.

"I think, after all is said and done, the right person will be in control. Whether that is Joss is still too soon to tell."

"And until then you will serve him?" I asked.

He nodded. "Of course I will, he saved my life."

That was surprising to hear. Other than myself, which was for selfish reasons, I never heard of Neil saving someone. "Oh? When was that?"

"About a year ago now. Some people were trying to kill me and he came out of nowhere and he saved me. Simple as that. Then I swore to serve him and showed him the fighting I could do, and he got even more intrigued. Been a trainer ever since." He took another bite of his sandwich. "Though I have to admit, you are a lot better at fighting than the other generals."

So that's what it was, Joss could read his mind and see that he was a talented fighter. It was all to make his generals even stronger. Now that I thought about it, that must have been why he picked the generals he did, because he could see in their minds what they were capable of. So everything he did was for his own selfishness. I should have figured that was his motive behind everything.

"What about you?" Dan asked. "What brought you here?"

"You mean other than Joss' men kidnapping me?"

He shrugged. "It was apparent you wanted to be here, otherwise you wouldn't have let yourself be captured. I see how you fight—you could have taken them all out. No, you wanted to be here, but whether it was because you wanted to pledge your loyalty to the Empire is another story."

He was smarter than I gave him credit for. "Fine. Yes, I wanted to be captured. I was working for the Republic, and I didn't like what they were doing. There was too much corruption, too much chaos. Wes is not doing what he is supposed to be doing, not following the laws. It might as well be an Emperor the way he is treating everyone. That is why I came here, because I knew that if I joined the Empire, then I could escape his tyranny." And that wasn't completely a lie, I really hated how my brother was operating things, but that didn't mean I liked how Joss did things either. Both of them were way past just being mildly corrupt.

"Interesting." He took another bite. "That is *quite* interesting, actually. That you would serve another just because of one bad egg."

"It's not just Wes, it is his generals as well. They will not stand up to him."

"Did you try to stand up against him?"

I nodded. "Many times, Came close to killing him, but someone always walked in and stopped me."

"And you weren't tried for treason?" he asked.

I shook my head. I should have been more careful as to what I was saying. Usually when one tried to kill an official, especially the Chancellor himself, they would be arrested. I couldn't explain to him he was my brother, that I was a Sanshlian, and we were from the future.

"No, Wes and I go way back. He wouldn't do that to me. Besides, he knew I would never go through with it. Though, I think that is unwise on his part. If Joss ordered me to, I would kill him without a second thought," I explained, hoping that was enough.

"That's good to hear, I suppose. But what if he told you to kill me?"

I gave him a look. This conversation took a surprising turn. It almost felt like talking to Lance. We were open with each other, jesting almost with our words. "Why would Joss order me to do that?"

"Just answer the question."

I stared at him a moment longer. He was serious. I shrugged. "You're the one person I can't kill. At least not yet anyway. If you fear he will order your death, then you should stop training me. Because if he gave the orders, and I could succeed, I wouldn't hesitate. He is my Emperor after all, I take orders from him and never look back."

Dan let out a laugh. "You are an interesting character. I can't wait to see what else you have in store for me."

I had no idea what he meant by that. I just admitted that I would kill him if it was ordered of me and he laughed it off. I wanted to know who this man was, and why he was so keen on figuring me out.

"What do you think of your trainer?" Joss asked as he had ordered me to his room. It was simple, as it was just one of many ship quarters. I had thought it would be a little bigger, but this was the start of the Empire after all.

I shrugged. "What about him? His training or him personally?"

"How about both?" Joss said, looking a bit amused.

"His training is extraordinary, I have met no one with such power. He is strong. He has beat me countless times without breaking a sweat. As you know, that is not an easy feat."

"And?" he asked, wanting me to go further.

I sighed. Talking about Dan felt complicated, even though it wasn't something that should be. He was just different and I couldn't quite place my finger on it.

"And he is a strange man. He keeps wanting to know more about me. I don't trust him, yet something inside me wants to. I don't understand who he is or what he wants, but I want to learn from him and that is all I know," I answered. There was no point in lying, it would achieve nothing with Joss. He could read minds and knew that I would feel this way about him. Joss knew me all too well, unfortunately.

Joss tapped his desk. "Interesting."

"How did you even come across him?" I asked. Because it wasn't like Joss to just pick up some random person. He must have had a reason. He was a talented trainer, yes, but to have him as close as this, training me of all people. There was an ulterior motive behind it, something that I couldn't quite piece together.

Joss stood up and looked out on the space-shield. "Random luck, I supposed. Stumbled across him because of one of the generals. He pointed out how excellent Dan was at fighting, and I decided he would make a great trainer. That really is it."

"Okay," I said, but honestly didn't believe him. I wouldn't press further on the subject though, if Joss wasn't going to tell me anything. "I also told him I would kill him if ordered and he didn't even care. He just laughed. I found that to be odd. Usually when I tell a person, I would kill them without a thought, they fear me or at least get mad. Dan did neither of those things, then again he knows how to take me down if need be."

"Which is why you are training with him." Joss turned back to me and smiled. "Speaking of which, what did Jack think when you were about to put a bullet in his head all those years ago?"

I narrowed my eyes. *Why was he bringing that up now? I*

cleared my throat. "You already know. He was about to kill me if I didn't lower the gun. There were snipers all around. He never trusted me in the slightest. He knew I was an Imperial."

"But he did after that."

I didn't answer. I didn't want to since he already knew everything that there was to be said about Jack.

Joss slapped me across the face. I didn't even resist it. I knew it was coming.

"What did we agree about him?"

"To not think about him or love him. I'm sorry sir, you brought him up and caught me off guard."

"Don't let it happen again," he snarled. I wondered what his genuine hatred for Jack was. It couldn't have just been because I went behind his back. It had to do with loyalty, or maybe jealousy. I wasn't sure.

"Yes sir."

It would be hard, I knew, when I saw Jack again, to have to turn my back on him. But it would be all right. I would suffer so we could be together again.

If this mission didn't kill me first.

And I knew Jack would do the same for me. It was apparent after he worked with the Empire just to guarantee my safety, although everyone had lied to him. He should have known better, but after everything that had happened, I understood why he did it.

"As for your training, keep working with Dan. He should be able to train you in every area that you are weak. Speaking of which, since you are a Sanshlian, have you started harnessing any of the powers that are given to the Illusionist?" Joss asked.

I hesitated. The only power I had was my strength, healing, and being able to hide my thoughts. And I didn't want him to know the last part.

"No. I don't know how to harness my powers or even use them. Other than strength and healing. I know that they are there but I have no one to train me," I answered.

He stared at me for a couple of moments, then nodded. "Fine. I will figure something out. You said that the others from the future gained powers as well?"

I nodded. "Yes they did. I presume all that were in that room and thrown in the past have gained powers, excluding the two of us as we were already Sanshlian, sir."

"It will be interesting to go against them. We will need you to master your powers for sure if we want to gain control."

"In actuality, that was another reason I didn't figure out my powers. I didn't want my brother using me for them, as he was used me to find Sanshli," I explained. "I also didn't know if he would even let me use my powers. He fears me more than anything. It was why he kept me close and under watchful supervision."

"Good, always thinking things through. But now, knowing who your father is, aren't you interested in how powerful you can become?"

I thought for a moment. It never occurred to me I could be as powerful as him, as I had never met the man. I wondered if I had the book, if I could learn the same illusions as him, to take over the universe as he did. Not that I wanted to, but the power intrigued me.

Was that the only way I could take him down? Destroy Nygard once and for all? At least, that was the plan.

"I am."

Joss' lips curled into a smile. "Well, we will have to start your training as soon as we are on Anosira."

"Why not now?"

He laughed. "Because if something goes wrong, I don't want to be stuck in the middle of space when you blast a hole through the ship."

I didn't think of that. If I had no idea how to harness my powers, it would be safest if I wasn't in space. "Good thinking. I can wait until we are planet side."

He turned and waved me off. "Now, back to your physical training. I need you to be the perfect servant."

I bowed. "Of course, sir."

Chapter 9

I didn't realize how much I missed Anosira until I laid my eyes on it. It was as beautiful as ever. The buildings were different, as the New Capital had not been founded yet. But that didn't change its uniqueness, its grandeur. As we glided over the tops of the mountains and forest, I took a deep breath. I got to see it again; I got to see nature again. For a year I had been stuck in that prison my brother made for me, never seeing nature like this. Now I felt almost free.

Keyword there: *almost*.

I knew that Joss was monitoring me. I knew that I would be under surveillance constantly, mainly by reading my mind. But that didn't mean it was any worse than how my brother had treated me. At least here I could move around and be free—Joss knew that if I tried anything, I understood he would kill me on the spot. There was no escaping him. He had waited a year to kidnap me, but that was only because of where Wes had me at all times. Inside the palace. Though I'm sure if he wanted to, he could have captured me before now. He was waiting until I came on my own. Or, at least, somewhat on my own.

We landed, and I started down the ramp with Dan, my only belongings being the clothes Joss had lent to me and my pocket-watch. After everything, Joss didn't take it away from me even though he must have known I had it since it was on my persons when he captured me. He could have taken it then, but I was thankful he didn't.

As we walked towards the palace, Dan said that we were to meet with the Emperor in his office. Joss must have hurried before us so he could meet up with the other generals before I could step out of the vehicle.

I knew where his office in the palace was, but I let Dan think he was guiding me. It would be hard to explain how I would know where everything was without having to expose the truth about what was going on or who I once was. Or will be, I guess. Time travel made everything confusing, something I was still pondering after all this time.

I thought about asking Dan if he knew who I was, but I didn't know how to broach such a topic. I also didn't know if Joss wanted him to have such knowledge and I didn't need to get into more trouble than I already was in. I supposed if he knew, he would have said something already. That or Joss was testing me and wanted to know how long I could keep such a secret to myself. I wouldn't let him have that satisfaction though, I wouldn't let him tease me like that.

We ventured through the palace. Things looked about the same as they did in the future, other than some different decorations scattered about here and there. The layout was the same, and that was all that mattered. I wondered if they built the underground tunnels yet or if this was before their time. I would have to ask Joss later. Or stumble across them once again. I was good at stumbling across such things.

We stepped into Joss' office, which was the same office I was used to, but decorated differently. Same coloring, oddly enough. I thought for sure many Emperors would have changed the style of the room to suit their aesthetic preference. It could have just been him, wanting the same as he had in the future, or they could have just not changed the red coloring. Either way, it made me forget I was in the past for a moment.

Joss was already there, waiting with three others. They had to be all three generals; Tom, Laura, and Pete. But who was who, I had no idea. They were each different, just as David and Will were. I'm sure he would introduce me to them eventually, and their identity didn't matter to me. I preferred not to have to talk to Tom, though the moment he opened his mouth I could probably conclude it was him.

"Myra, please, take a seat," Joss gestured to a seat. I sat down and Dan sat next to me. "I thought it would be best to bring you all here to understand that Myra has come back to the Empire and will help us destroy the Second Republic once again."

"I thought you captured her. Now she is on our side?" one of the two men said. He had dark blonde hair and was cleanly shaven. He could be Pete, could be Tom. I wasn't sure yet, although he didn't use any profanity, so it was probably Pete.

"I did, but she admitted to me that she saw the errors in her ways. She is back and I know that to be a fact." He licked his lips. "As I know that all of your loyalty is to me and me alone."

"So you think we can trust her?" the woman said. Laura, that one I knew to be a fact. She still had that frigid expression she always had. That and she was the only woman I knew from the past that could have been here. "Are you that trusting of her?"

"I am. As you know I can read her mind. Myra has seen the error in her ways and with Wes' destruction throughout the universe, she knows the importance of the Empire and what greatness it will soon bring."

I glanced over at Dan. If Joss could say aloud in Dan's presence that he could read minds, that meant he knew about our powers. *So*, I wondered, *does that mean he knows what I am?*

"After everything, you finally came crawling back, eh Myra?" the blonde man said again.

Raised my eyebrow. "Got a bone to pick with me?"

He shrugged. "Just seems like you get out of the shit you do pretty easily. Can't help but wonder how."

"Oh, believe me, I get to pay the price of my sins. Joss

has made sure of that."

The blonde let a grin appear on his face. "Well, I would definitely like to see that in action."

"That's enough." Joss stopped our bickering, just as always. "I want you five to get along. I don't want to hear you acting like children ever again. I don't want to deal with your fights, your bickering, your child-like behavior. For once in your life, act like you are generals. That includes you, Myra."

"Yes sir," I said. I saw Laura hide a grin. Usually Neil held me in his favor, he would only take his anger out on the others. Now that wasn't the case.

"Okay. Now," he pointed to one of the men. "General Tim Nevo. General Logan Pale. General Jane Doresmith. You three are dismissed. I need to catch Myra up on a few things. We will meet again in a few hours and go through any information Myra has for us about the Republic."

The three of them bowed and left. I kept my eye on the two men and tried to figure out which was which. From what I could remember, Thomas and Pete both hated me equally, though Tom hated me a little more. Both of them would pick on me though, so I had no idea which could be which. I turned back to the Emperor as they left.

"Which one is Tom and which one is Pete? It is hard to tell," I commented. I then realized Dan was still with us and tapped my mouth. "Oh, I mean—"

Joss waved me off. "It's fine, he knows that we are from the future."

I found this admission to be odd, as the Neil I knew

would never give some random person information that they didn't have to know. That meant there was something going on with him, more than I realized. And as to what that was, it would be awhile before I found out, if ever.

"I'm surprised you didn't notice," Joss went on. "Neither of them were Tom, he is away on a mission. He won't be back for a while."

I felt my heart skip a beat. "Jack?"

"Tim is Jack and Logan is Pete. I'm surprised you didn't notice by the way he was looking at you. I guess you were just so used to them glaring at you that you weren't paying enough attention to them. It wouldn't have occurred to you that one of them was Jack."

"What can I say, I am used to scowling. I usually just turn my back on them and don't give them any attention."

"I bet you that do," Joss stood up. "And he is waiting outside for you right now."

My heart felt like it was being crushed by Joss' fist. But I wouldn't let that affect me. I couldn't, not when it could cost me the end of this war. "I won't do anything you haven't ordered, sir."

"Just making sure," he glanced at Dan. He had been silent, listening to our conversation. I wondered how much he knew of the feuds between me and the others. "Dan, I presume Myra is doing well as she trains with you, that she isn't causing you any problems."

"She is doing well, yes. We still have a lot to work on, but we will get there, eventually."

"Good to hear. Must drive her insane that she can't beat you. See, she hasn't ever been defeated before," he glanced over at me, curious to learn my reaction. I didn't give him the honor of seeing me as weak as I was with Dan. I held my head high, as if I was taking this training to become stronger. Which I was, but it still ate away at my pride that Dan could beat me so easily.

Dan replied. "Then you must have had some weak people working for you, Joss. There is so much she doesn't know."

I shot Dan a look. He enjoyed joking around like this, just because he was so skilled. He knew I hated it, but I couldn't do anything about it. Though I didn't understand why my usual survival reflexes egging me to kill him had gone away and now, I just wanted to learn more from him. I felt comfortable around him even though I didn't know much about him. I learned never to trust anyone, yet here I was, putting my faith in him, that he would teach me everything I need to know.

"I presume you will further her teachings to strengthen her powers as well?"

I looked at Dan. What did he mean by that? Did he mean that Dan knew about my powers, that he knew enough to train me? Was he a Sanshlian as well? I knew that since the Emperor had been a Sanshlian that they were still out there, thousands of years later. Could Dan also be a descendent of a Sanshlian?

"Yes I will. I am looking forward to that. I want to see what her powers are."

He didn't know enough to know who I was, but knew

that I had powers. Interesting. Maybe he didn't have powers but was always close-by to the Emperors, as they needed to be trained using their powers as well. Joss had once said his parents included a mind reader and an illusionist. I guess someone had to teach them.

"I'm glad I will be able to control them," I added. "Wes wouldn't let me train with anyone, and with him watching my every move, it was kind of hard to do anything."

"But at least you had Lance, or am I incorrect?" Joss added.

I felt my cheeks redden, but not out of embarrassment. I was mad that he kept bringing that up, wanting to hurt me more and more.

"Calm down, Myra, I was only joking. Now." He sat back down. "Tell me about what your brother has in store for us."

"He is planning on attacking Ttkas. He wants to destroy their military bases, and most of their capital."

"When?" Joss asked.

I shrugged. "I'm not sure, but I know it's bound to happen soon. He is gathering troops as we speak."

Joss rubbed the scruff on his chin. "We haven't even contacted them. It's too early. They are still with the Second Republic."

"I know that, but Wes doesn't care. He wants to destroy them before they even commit treason. It's sickening. I even confronted him about it, but he didn't care. It was where his wife was killed and he didn't care that so many people would die, and it's all because of his clouded judgment. Not even Lance or Alan can, or will, stop him."

"Which is why you are here."

I nodded. "Nothing that the Empire has done has been that of wrongdoing. Wes is dragging this into an even darker time than we can ever imagine. We must stop him and bring order back to the universe. Through the Empire, I pledge my loyalty, as I always have. I will not turn away. Give me a mission, I am yours to use."

Joss' lips turned into a smile. "I'm glad to hear that Myra, even though I know you are just trying to make me trust you. You need not go above and beyond. You don't need to kiss my ass, though I won't complain if you do."

"Sorry sir," I responded automatically. I was used to apologizing, even before everything with discovering my Sanshlian roots. I wondered how many times I had told him I was sorry, that I meant it or if it was just a reflexive response I was used to giving.

"But as for this news of Wes attacking Ttkas, we need to act first. I want you and Dan to... *persuade* the representative to align with us."

With the word 'persuade', I could feel my adrenaline rush. I hadn't been on a mission for such a long time, or at least not one assigned to me. I was still on the mission to take down Nygard, but this was different. This was what all my years of training prepared me for, situations where I got to feel like the old me again, although I didn't know if that was a good or a bad thing. I hadn't been the best sort of person, as Wes was quick to point out again and again. I had even killed my Father's friend, basically our uncle-like figure growing up. I was under orders by the Emperor to take down the head of the PAE operation and our uncle stood in my way. He could have run, I gave him the chance. Instead he told me I was breaking my father's heart and then I shot him point blank. It was his fault, I told myself, repeatedly, during nights that I couldn't sleep. He should have run when I gave him the chance.

But that was a long time ago, and I had killed hundreds of more men like him, ones that worked for the PAE, committing terrorist-like attacks, yet thinking I was the bad guy for stopping them. What they were doing was sowing chaos, it wouldn't bring back the Empire, it would only bring them death.

And now it was happening all over again. The Second Republic was causing chaos, and I had to help snuff it out. Well, at least appear like I was aiding in quelling it. What I was looking for was Sanshli.

"And by persuade, you mean…" I asked.

"Don't kill him, but make sure he will never betray us," Joss clarified. He knew he had to mention not to kill him, as he had learned that mistake long ago. I needed specifics, otherwise my strength got the better of me.

I nodded, happy to be doing some kind of work. Wes had me cooped up in a box for so long, I needed to threaten someone like this, torture if necessary.

And I was excited about it.

I had faith that it would be easy, especially if Dan was with me. I knew I wouldn't have to worry, that he would have my back if anything went wrong.

Believe me, something always went wrong. I was cursed like that. Even the simplest missions always went haywire. I could always count on that.

"When do you want us to leave?" I asked.

"In the morning, as soon as possible. As for now, deal with Jack waiting outside the door. He's still waiting. I want you to end it now, Myra. Then Dan will take you to train some more with him."

Dan and I stood up. I bowed. "Yes, sir."

Chapter 10

Just as Joss said, Jack was waiting outside in the corridor for me. I sighed, not wanting to deal with the ache in my chest. I had been thinking of him for over a year, wanting to feel his arms around me, kissing my head gently, but now that I was near him, I still could have that if only not prohibited from seeing him. I should have figured, as Joss was never the sympathetic kind. I had been going behind his back, though, so I deserved it in my eyes.

I turned to Dan, who was watching Tim. I wondered what he was thinking and why he was studying him like that, as they must have worked together already. "Dan, can I have a moment? I will meet you in the training room."

He smiled. "Sure thing. Just be careful, all right? Don't do anything stupid."

I raised an eyebrow. "You don't know me well enough to think I would do something stupid."

"Joss has told me all about you."

Just as I had expected. I wondered what all Joss had told him about me. "Ah. Goodie."

He waved as he left towards the training room. I took a deep breath and faced General Tim Nevo. Faced Jack.

As everyone else, he changed bodies, which was strange to know I loved a man with a different body. His hair was a dark black, cut a lot closer to his head than I had ever seen it. His blue eyes stared at me, waiting for me to acknowledge his existence. He looked like a puppy, waiting for someone to throw him a bone. Though this puppy was once a ruthless crime lord on Recar, one of the most successful in all the time Recar had been ruled by crime lords. Yet here he was, helping the Empire. Times had changed, but that look on his face never did.

Damn, he was as cute as he always was.

"Arcadia." Tim approached me as Dan left. "Can we go somewhere?" He glanced over to the closed door that led to Joss' office. So he was afraid of him as well. "Somewhere away from here?"

I nodded. "Yeah. Let's."

He grabbed my hand and led me towards the conference hallway. His hand was warm in mine, and he smelled of cinnamon. Quickly we went into a room, and he closed the door behind us.

"I don't know what Joss told you, but you know who I am right?" he asked.

I nodded. "Jack."

He tried to approach me and wrap his arms around me, but I stepped away from. His arms returned to his sides, and he let out a sigh. "He told you not to love me again, didn't he?"

I shook my head. "No, it's not that. This last year I realized that I don't love you, Jack. My loyalty has always been to the Emperor and the Emperor alone. I can't turn my back on him. I can't give my heart to someone yet my loyalty to another."

It was a lie, a ridiculous lie that I knew he wouldn't believe. He had never left my side when we were on Sanshli, when I could feel my sanity slipping away as those voices become louder and louder. He promised to always be there for me, so for me to say my loyalty was to the Emperor and him alone. After what he did to me, I wondered if he would believe that.

"I don't believe you, Arcadia. You love me, and I know that. Joss is making you lie to me, I can see that in your eyes. Please, just— "

"No. This is my decision and mine alone. And my name isn't Arcadia, it's Myra. This is who I am now, this is who I should have been all along. All the times we were together I realize were wrong. I realize I shouldn't have betrayed the Emperor like that and it will never happen again," I said, trying not to let my genuine emotions show. Jack was as good as I was at reading people. If I let them show, he would notice right away.

Tim stared at me, his blue eyes feeling like they were piercing my soul. "If... If he told you to kill me, would you?"

At first I didn't answer. I didn't want to because I knew the truth. "Yes. I would."

He opened his mouth to respond, but there was nothing to say. I had betrayed him, I knew, but it was the only way. It was the only thing I could do to get him to stop threatening Jack, the only thing I could do to keep him safe.

"Well. All right then. I will leave you alone."

I nodded. "Thank you."

He left the conference room, and I stood there, staring at the empty doorway for a moment, taking deep breaths. I couldn't show weakness, that was how I had lived my life with the Emperor, and through the Kamps. I couldn't let this hurt me, I had to move on.

Yet no matter how many times I repeated that to myself, my heart still hurt.

After I regained my senses, I headed to where Dan was waiting for me. Maybe with all the frustration I had pinned up, I could defeat him by letting it all out. Probably not, but it was worth a shot.

As I headed towards the training room, I tried taking my mind off Jack by thinking about Wes and the others. I wondered how long it would take for them to figure out I was gone. Wes would think I ran off, gone back to my old ways, which I did in a way. Lance would be furious or heartbroken, I wasn't sure which, nor did I care at this point. Alan's hatred would just rise and he would want to kill me even more. I shook my head at just the thought of them. They didn't understand the real game that was being played here. They didn't understand what was at stake.

Nygard needed to be destroyed, only then could peace be restored to the galaxy.

I knew Nygard was evil from all the stories Father had told us growing up. He had destroyed Sanshli and its people, seeking revenge for his people who had been suppressed, but the problem was that none of them wanted to gain the power that he so craved. None wanted to cave into temptation. So he killed many of the Illusionists, as they were in his way.

Now, the question was, if I was trying to master my powers, where did that put me? Was I evil as well? Or was it only natural to need to be powerful to take down Nygard?

This was a question I hadn't brought up to Violet, as I didn't want to know the answer. I had a feeling that was why she didn't want to teach me about my powers: for fear I would turn into Nygard. I couldn't promise that the power wouldn't get to my mind. I had done so many terrible things in the past already.

It wasn't like what my brother was doing would bring peace either. In fact, I was sure it was just going to bring destruction. He was such an idiot, more so than he had ever been. He needed to take a lesson from me on how to control his emotions, how to see the goal and let nothing impede that.

Or maybe that was his problem, that his goal was so corrupt that nothing could stop him.

I walked into the training room to find Dan working

with Jane. Apparently, she wanted to train as well. I watched as Dan flipped her onto the mat.

Chuckling, I approached them. "Seems you have a lot to learn as well, Jane was it?"

She narrowed her eyes, an icy stare that I was used to. "Shut it, I would like to see you do better."

"How about it, then? You and I duel. It's been a while, hasn't it? At least, since last time I defeated you."

She let out a deep breath, as if holding herself back from hitting my face with the notion that I wouldn't block it. "Fine. I've grown a lot since we last fought. Don't think you can defeat me so easily."

"We will see about that." I glanced over at Dan, who had remained silent. "Is it all right with you?"

He waved me on. "Oh, go for it. I'm not going to stand in the middle of a catfight. I learned that lesson long ago."

I smiled. It was so easy to work with Dan, he knew what to say and not to push me. I liked that, and wished everyone would be like him. Then I wouldn't have to kill so many people.

"Ready?" Jane asked.

I raised my hands in the new stance Dan showed me. Jane, or Laura, always used a boxing technique, her fist ready and blocking her face.

She was the first to start the fight. She punched with her right hand, then her left, but I blocked both attacks. I swung my leg as she punched again, leaving her core wide open. I swung my arm, but she regained her stance and blocked it.

Jane kept at me, punch after punch, but I was quick to counter each attack. She swung high, and I ducked, and backed up as she switched to a low swing. Before I could regain my balance, she swung and hit me right in the jaw.

There was a slight smile on her face.

"I didn't know the Ice Queen smiled. I guess you must hate me enough to find joy in hitting me."

"Oh, you bet."

"Well, then. Maybe I should step up my game." I lunged forward, taking swing after swing at her, but she dodged each of these attacks and punched back, once in the ribs and the second in my jaw again.

"I'm waiting, Myra. Show me what you've got."

I rubbed away the blood from the cut against my lip. "Fine. But you've asked for it."

Before she knew it was coming, I kicked her leg, punched her jaw, and kicked her leg again, making her lose part of her balance. As she tried to regain it again, I elbowed her in the stomach, grabbed her arm, and hit my palm straight into her shoulder blade.

She backed off for a moment and regained her balance. She swung at me again, but I blocked it and countered the attack, though she blocked that as well. I ducked down and slammed my fist into her stomach. As she bent over, I grabbed her arm and pulled her forward, kneeing her straight in the nose.

Pulling out of my hold, she swung back, her eyes furious. Now she was attacking out of anger, making her fighting sloppy. I blocked her attacks and punched her in the nose again. Blood ran down her face, and she wiped it away. Her skin was turning red as she struck at me again and again, but I ducked out of the way of her attack and kicked her straight in the stomach.

She hit the ground, and as quickly as I could, I jumped on her and let my fist come centimeters from her face. I grinned.

"I think I won this one."

"Get off of me," she snarled. I got off, not wanting to summon the wrath of Jane. She got up and hit me with her shoulder as she left the training room, holding her hand to her bloody nose in bitter disgrace.

I turned to Dan and smiled. "Sore loser. She never liked losing to me."

"I don't think it's just you, I don't think she enjoys losing to anyone. But she seems to get angrier when it's against you."

I grabbed a towel to wipe the blood off my lip. "She usually won't train with me ever. It has been a very long time since she has let me go against her in a fight. I'm surprised she didn't make an excuse this time."

"She probably didn't think you have been training."

"Well," I began. "She should have known better."

"Should we continue your lessons?" Dan asked.

I nodded. "Yes, let's."

After working with Dan for a while, I retired for the day. We were to go to Ttkas in the morning and I didn't want to be completely drained, although I knew I could catch up on my strength on the ship. Though, with him on the ship, I had a feeling my training would continue uninterrupted for a time. I had a lot to learn, and once we were back from Ttkas, he promised that he would start training me in learning how to use my Sanshlian powers. I still wasn't sure how he would do that, but I trusted him. Joss trusted him, so I would too.

I made my way down the corridors to my old quarters. I presumed that was where I would stay, and after Dan told me the room number, I knew it was it. Room 582, just as always. I had that number seared into my brain.

Letting the door slide open, I found the room to be how it used to. Ordinary and not decorated. Just how I liked it. The couch and bed were different, but everything else was the same. The color, the layout, all of it. Including the mirror that hung in the room.

"Everything is set." I said as I sat down in front of the mirror. I still felt as if I was crazy talking into the mirror, but I got over that long ago. "I am being sent to Ttkas to stop Wes' attack."

Violet appeared in front of my image. *"Good. You know where to look?"*

I nodded as I took off my boots. "Of course. Inside the brick, right?"

"Theoretically."

"That sounds reassuring."

"You know how these things play out, you know how things can go wrong."

"I know all too well," I sighed. Everything always seemed to go wrong when I was on a mission. It was like my destiny to have everything become more and more complicated. "What happens when I find this thing? What do I do then?"

"Then you go looking for Sanshli. Then you stop this."

It sounded so much easier than it was. To say 'stop this' made it sound like some simple task. That was not the case, not when this legend had been going on for so long, jumping through time. It was anything but simple.

"Destroy the book and Nygard you mean?" I asked.

"Yes."

"Fine," I stretched. "I need to rest for a bit. Long day of planning tomorrow, along with avoiding the man I love, and lying to a vindictive leader whose ass I have to kiss. It all takes its toll, you know."

She gave me her usual look when I put things so bluntly. As if I needed to hide my true thoughts or something. I wondered if she knew the things I had done in the past, when I was working for the Empire, or if she only knew my life from the moment the ghosts entered my mind on Sanshli. Could she see my thoughts at all times like Joss could, or only when I communicated to her? I hated how so many people could see inside my mind if that was the case. What was Sanshli like in the olden days, when there were so many mind readers? Did no one have any privacy, or did they all learn to shield their minds against one another's prying thoughts? It seemed like a useless power if that was the case. But then again, I wasn't there, I didn't know the entire story.

"Goodnight sweetheart."

I smiled. "Goodnight Mother."

As she disappeared, I leaned back on the couch. There

was so much to be done still. This was only the beginning. I thought back on when this whole quest started, when my brother kidnapped me and made me look for those books with the keys Father had left us. Would it be the same as that? Running around the galaxy blind, looking for some elusive legend. I didn't have Lance this time to help me decode things, all I had was my mother, though that would be a little more beneficial, since she was the one who hid the clues. I still didn't understand why she couldn't just tell me where Sanshli was, but I guess the location didn't follow physics, so unless you were keeping track on where the planet was moving, it was rather hard. Not to mention she wasn't physical, but just a ghost. She wasn't actually here, but just a resonance through time. I could never touch her, therefore I could never be with her.

I did not understand how that even worked, if she was alive in spirit or if it was some prerecording. The whole concept of ghosts and how they worked in general, if one believed in such things, was also a mystery to me. I couldn't help to ponder such things, as I felt I was surrounded by them, both figuratively and literally in the sense of my mother.

Thinking of ghosts made me think of Father, my Father on Garvner. I wished I could see him again, have him help me, comfort me for all the things that had happened since his death. If he hadn't died, if we had escaped that night, it all would have been different. I would have been prepared for what I needed to do, I would have known the truth.

But there was no point of thinking of such things. I had to move forward, I had to keep going so that peace would be restored, so I had the possibility of living a life I wanted, not the life that everyone else was forcing me to live. A prophecy, a servant, a prisoner. All I wanted to be was just me. Was that too much to ask?

A knock sounded at the door. I moaned, hoping it wasn't Tim, or Joss, or anyone. Maybe it was the wrong door, maybe they would go away. I waited a second, but whoever it was knocked again. I got up and used my power to sense who it was through the walls. To my surprise, it was Dan.

"Dan?" I asked as I opened the door and he walked in. "Thought you said I didn't need guarding. Why are you here?"

"Don't worry, I'm not here to guard you. I was just curious how you were doing, what you were thinking."

I studied him, not sure what he was asking. "Excuse me?"

"About Jack. What are your feelings towards him?" Dan sat down on my couch. I gave him a suspicious look. What had Joss told him about Jack? And why did he care?

"What are you talking about?"

"Joss said you used to be lovers, but he forbade you from ever seeing him again. Why is that?"

I watched him, wondering if I could tell what his deal was. It was none of his business and after these past few days, he should have known that I wouldn't be very keen on letting him ask these kinds of questions. Hell,

Thomas and I used to get in fist fights over Jack. "What's it to *you*?"

Dan shrugged, as if he wanted me to talk. "I'm just curious. I am your trainer."

"That means nothing. My thoughts are none of your business. Are you spying on me on Joss' orders? Does he think he can get into my head through you? Wanting to check to make sure I'm not lying to him somehow?"

"No, he's not. I am here on my own. I saw your pain while we were training, I could see that you took it out on Jane. You are struggling and most people want to talk about it. I know you have had no one to talk to in the past, so I wanted to help."

"That's a lie. You don't know me, you will never know me. Don't think just because I like you training me, that I am nicer to you than others that I will *ever* open up to you. All you need to know is that I serve the Emperor, and he owns my loyalty and my life. The scars I have inside are just a payment I have to give due to my ignorance. I learned my lesson the hard way, Joss saw to that."

"A scar, just like the mark on your wrist?" he asked. I shifted, placing my other hand on top of my glove. There was no way he would have ever seen it. "What is that?"

I narrowed my eyes. "How do you know about the mark? There is no way you could have seen it."

"You took your gloves off once during training. I saw the lines. What are they?"

I pointed at the door. "Out. Now."

"Myra, I—" he began, but I shook my head.

"Out. Now!"

He stood up and nodded his head. "I'm sorry Myra, I didn't mean to hurt you. I just want to be here for you."

"That will never be possible. Go rest up, we will leave in the morning."

He nodded and left me in my quarters. My heart was racing. Why would anyone care other than Jack? No one has ever, other than David, but he was naïve and thought I was innocent in the beginning. This man knew everything about me and still wanted to know more.

And I did not understand why that was.

I lay back on the couch and let my mind drift off to somewhat pleasanter places. The mystery could wait another day. I needed my rest. I needed to prepare for the mission that was at hand.

Chapter 11

Ttkas was only a three-day trip away. Ships moved slower compared to the future, but that didn't mean that it still wasn't that far away. As ordered, I traveled with Dan; he was like my coach and guard all in one. I never thought I would need coaching again, as I had mastered many fighting techniques and could even beat the top-ranking military officers for both the Pandronan Empire and the Second Republic. I hadn't had so much trouble sparring before and it made me curious why. There had to be something else to it, something that I wasn't seeing. There was no way a normal person could beat me at fighting like he could.

I thought about asking him outright, but learned that through the years, asking for the truth hadn't gotten me anywhere. I was constantly lied to, no one spoke a word of truth to me. Sure, I was good at lying, good at hiding the fears inside of me. But that didn't matter, Neil could read my mind, and he knew everything.

I felt foolish for acting like a child when he asked me how I felt. I wanted to apologize, but I feared he would try to pry into my personal life again. So I did the only thing I knew how to do, and that was pretend it never happened. Healthy way to deal with things, right?

He also didn't bring it up, which surprised me. Maybe he learned not to mess with me. I would be surprised if that was the case. We had already argued a few times about him asking me questions about my past. What part of don't ask me didn't he understand?

We only took a small Class Two ship, which only the two of us were navigating. There was no reason to bring anyone else since this was a mission involving slipping by the Republic and getting the representative of Ttkas on our side. It wouldn't be difficult, I knew, as none of these representatives had any backbone, and their history has remained unchanged on that score. A simple threat, a few punches in the stomach, and he would be ours. Just like always.

One downside of being on such a small ship was that there was no training room. We had the mess hall, and that was it. So we moved the table out of the way and fought. Without a mat, I might add. Dan didn't seem to mind, though he wasn't the one getting thrown to the ground.

Again, good thing I could heal so fast.

As I hit the ground, I felt my shoulder blade crack. I let

out a brief yelp in pain. Damn, I should have been more careful.

Dan's eyes widened as he too heard the noise. "Are you okay?"

I pulled myself up, whimpering just a little bit. "Snapped my shoulder blade. Should be fine in a few hours."

"What?"

I shook my head. "I can heal fast, it should be fine. Meanwhile, we should go over the plan for getting close to the representative."

He helped me to the chair. I may heal quickly, but that didn't mean that it didn't hurt. I grimaced as the back of the chair touched the broken bone. "Do we have alcohol? I think alcohol would be lovely right about now."

"Are you even really old enough for that?" Dan asked.

I gave him a look, letting him know I didn't care, not to mention he just broke my shoulder blade.

"Right." Dan nodded and went to the pantry to get whatever he could find. He came back with a bottle of vodka. Fitting since we were heading to Ttkas. We could grab some more when we landed.

He handed me the bottle, and I opened it and chugged. I hadn't consumed alcohol for a while. The bite hit me, and I started coughing.

"You should be careful, that's not a proof for chugging. It's on the high end." Dan sat down across from me. "Hand me the bottle."

I passed it on, and he took a quick sip. "Wow, this tastes like crap."

"It helps though." I took another sip. "So, have any ideas of how we will get close to the representative? I have a feeling he has a bunch of guards stationed around him with the threat of war looming across the galaxy."

Dan shrugged. "It is hard to say at the moment. We need to hack into his schedule, see where he will be, and plan from there."

"Got a tablet? I could get into it online."

Dan grabbed a tablet. I quickly ran through it, digging into Tkas' database. It was easy, they needed to increase their security. I made a mental note to tell Joss that when we got back. "There, found his schedule. For when we land, it should be his day of meetings with the senate. There's a brief hour where he is in his office doing paperwork, or god-knows-what. We should plan to sneak in then."

"You think it will be that simple?" Dan raised an eyebrow. I laughed.

"It's Tkas, of course it will be. They may be known for their military weapons, but as for their security currently, it's not that great. Facilities, yes, but the rest of the city is pretty bad. Just don't get caught. What they lack in security, they regain in harsh treatment to those they arrest."

"Good to know. Are you sure your shoulder will be fine by then?"

I nodded. "Yeah, it will be. Don't worry about it. Just need to sit here for a bit, let it stop hurting."

"Anything you need right now?"

"No, you can go rest. I will monitor the ship."

He nodded and got up to head to his quarters. I sighed, wanting to punch a hole in the wall. I should have been more careful when I hit the ground, now I just sat here with pain in my shoulder. At least it would go away eventually, and I would be ready before we landed.

Taking a deep breath, I focused on what I would need to do for the mission. It would just be a matter of time, then Ttkas would be under our control.

And then I could find the secret clue on Ttkas and find Sanshli. Only then would my mission be complete.

A day passed, and I was able to heal from my shoulder injury. We were almost to Ttkas, I could see the snowy planet coming up out of the space-shield. It surprised me how it didn't seem to have changed much, but I guess snow was snow. I knew many down there would disagree, that there were different distinct types of snow, but I didn't care about what they thought. I knew it was cold and covered everything and it was a pain to deal with.

Seeing the planet reminded me of Amanda. She had met her end on this planet, or at least would meet her end in the future. I wondered, when all was said and done, whether she would be alive, or if her death was a set point in time. Both she and Father had met their end because of the Empire. Could this bring them back?

I shook my head. I didn't want to think of Father. I didn't want to get my hopes up, not when I had such a big task to finish before we could even go back to the future. I had to find Sanshli, I had to defeat Nygard somehow. It wouldn't be easy, and I doubted that I would survive after this was over. Even if I did, I could be sent to the past where I was from originally. There were too many variables and getting my hopes up would just be a weakness someone could exploit.

"Looks cold." Dan stepped next to me.

I nodded. "That it is. Bring a coat."

"Oh, I planned on that. Too bad we can't explore the planet, I bet it has some wonderful scenery."

"No, it doesn't. You can find snow on most planets with more picturesque settings. This is just a lump of ice that people who can't afford to leave stay on. The only option is to manufacture weapons with the metals they mine for, or else no one will trade with them. They will just be on their own and dissolve into nothing." I turned to face him. "Jane is from there. Gives you an idea of these people's personalities."

"Ah. I didn't realize she was from there. Must have some interesting stories."

I shrugged. "Not really. Her parents sold her to the military, and she became a lethal machine. Joss then hired her, and she went back and destroyed everything her parents ever had. That's why I call her the Ice Queen. Then again, I wouldn't have left any of them alive." Although that story was from the future, not this life, it fit her either way.

"A little harsh, don't you think?" he asked.

"No, not after what they did to her. But I'm not known for my generosity either."

"Well, that's interesting then. So if someone betrayed

you, tried to kill you, you would stop at nothing to destroy them?"

I watched him. He appeared to be sincere in his question, but I wasn't sure where it was coming from. Had he been hurt in his past and wanted to seek revenge? I wasn't sure, but I knew what I would do. "Yes. Of course, that is as long as Joss allows it."

Dan grinned. "That's good to hear. So you understand what revenge can do to a person."

It wasn't so much as a question rather than an understanding. I wondered what he could seek revenge for. "But it is very rare for someone to betray me, as I don't let anyone get close," I explained.

"What about Wes?"

I shook my head. "He was never close. And I left and am with the Empire now, so that answers that question."

"True, when you put it that way. We better report in to the planet's authorities, don't want them to suspect us."

"Oh, but that makes it even more fun." I laughed. "Yeah, we better check in and so they can give us a docking spot. Should land within two hours, and the representative has his break in four. We will be cutting it close, but it should work out fine."

Dan nodded and gestured to the cockpit. "After you."

We landed within two hours, just as I planned we would. The representative's office was about an hour away and we waited in line to get a ticket for the train that headed to the capital, as the port was not connected like in many other planets. It was cold, just as I figured it would be, and I couldn't believe how many people around us had a light jacket on. They shivered as they waited in line, their jacket riddled with holes. Poverty marked this planet, even under the Republic. I couldn't believe it, not after the Republic claiming that they would make sure food was at every table, and clothes on every person.

I wondered if it was better before we came along a year ago or if Wes made matters worse for them. It wouldn't surprise me, as he blames Ttkas for a good chunk of the war. He was making innocent people suffer. At least after today it would be a little better, that is, if Wes backed down once Ttkas was under our control. Most of the military weapons were on this planet. It would be suicide for his people to attack her once they sided with Joss.

We got on the train and I watched as we passed compact houses that looked as if they wouldn't be warm on a sunny day. And Wes would attack them, make them realize what he could do if they ever betrayed him. He was a fool to hurt so many innocent people.

I turned to Dan, wanting to ignore my feelings of sympathy. I hated feeling this way and didn't want to ever feel that way again. I didn't want to be reminded what was taken from me all those years ago, the family that I once loved. If Wes attacked, these children would face the same fate as us, if not worse.

"Something wrong?" Dan asked. I shook my head no as the train entered a tunnel into the mountain. The lights turned on as darkness now surrounded us.

"I'm fine. Just thinking about everything. It should all

be fine, though, so I shouldn't worry."

"And you have me with you, so you don't have to worry about getting captured." He grinned, as if I needed saving.

I glared at him. "I would be fine without you, Joss is just worried I might betray him. I never get caught without wanting to or having a plan to escape."

"Is that so? Then you let yourself be captured by Joss' men? And also, could have left Wes anytime you wanted?"

I stayed silent for a moment. That was true, I could have left at any time I wanted while under Wes' roof. But I wanted to know what he was doing, I wanted to get stronger in blocking my mind before facing Joss once again. I shrugged. "I was just curious about what Wes was doing, I could have left, that is true. And yes, I knew that Joss was waiting for me. Had to knock a few people out though, make it more believable, but I was in control the entire time and Joss knows that."

"Very interesting. I don't know if you are smart or so egotistic that you just think you are in charge."

I punched him in the arm. "I also don't lie so you can just shut up."

He laughed. "All right then, I will."

It wasn't much longer before we found ourselves in the capital. It was as sad as the rest of the planet was, without many tourists around. Everyone here either appeared to live on the planet or were here for business. The men in suits and trench coats I spotted near the Capital Building had to be the senators coming to talk to the representative. That meant we would talk to him before he meets with the senators. Perfect timing, he could claim independence right away and we would know if we were successful.

This was going perfectly. I could not wait.

I nodded to Dan towards the entry that we would need to take. He followed behind as we snuck past two guards.

"The back entry is this way, at least according to the schematics I found. There will be a guard or two waiting," I said.

"Leave the guards to me, I can take care of them."

I raised an eyebrow. "Oh? You mean I get to see you in action against someone other than me?"

"Can't let you hurt yourself before we get to the representative, now can I?"

"Very funny. The entrance is just up ahead. Have at it."

Dan nodded, and as we rounded the corner, three guards stood at the entrance. Dan was quick to attack before they noticed we were even there. I watched as with one hand he could knock them all to the ground. Even I wasn't able to do that. I still had a lot more training to learn from him, that was for sure.

Gesturing me to follow him inside, Dan grabbed a key card off one of the guards and we went into the capital. From what I memorized of the layouts, the representative's office was down the hall, turn right, turn left, the third door on the left. I led the way as we pushed past the workers. They didn't notice that we weren't supposed to be there. The key is acting like you belong.

Then no one notices that you aren't supposed to be there. At least, that's how it goes.

"Oi! You two! You aren't supposed to be here!" a man behind us yelled. I glanced back and sure enough one of the guards Dan had knocked out was awake and heading our way.

"Probably a wonderful time to run, wouldn't you say?" I asked Dan.

He nodded. "Go on ahead, I will take care of this."

"Got it. Just don't get captured, I don't want to have to come find you."

"I'll try my best." With that, he ran back towards the guard and I ran towards the room the Representative was in. I heard people calling out for the alarm to be sounded, so I knew I would have to act quick. If I waited, then the representative would be taken to somewhere they deemed safe. I couldn't wait that long.

I barged into the room to find the Representative hurrying towards a back exit. I pulled out my Class Two gun.

"Not so fast, Representative Allumas. I need to talk to you."

Chapter 12

"Wha—what do you want? Who are you? I have nothing of value, I'm just a puppet. I can't do anything." He was quick to think of excuses, which always showed that one was weak, that they knew that they couldn't defend themselves. It was their last resort, make the killer feel sympathetic towards them. This would be easier than I thought.

"My name is Myra and I come with a message from Emperor Joss himself." I didn't lower my weapon, knowing that at any chance he had, he would run off and summon the guards. Believe me, it has happened before. Many times, actually.

His eyes widened, fearful that I would kill him. It was the same look they all got when in dire straits, even if I didn't have a gun and wasn't ordered to kill them. I felt as if my power was coming back to me. My nickname as being the Emperor's Shadow would once again be restored. That made me excited, that it meant I could go back to how things were, which wasn't true. There was still so much more going on.

Allumas peered around, but didn't move. He probably wondered why his men hadn't come in here to stop me, and that was because Dan had them preoccupied outside. I had to give him credit where credit was due. He knew how to handle these situations, he wasn't just good at training, he was also good in the field.

The Representative turned back to me, realizing the only way to escape this was to do as I said. That I held his life in my hands and that if I wanted to kill him, I could. Unfortunately, Joss ordered me not to. "Don't kill me, please, I have done nothing to deserve it."

"I won't kill you as long as you do what I say." I motioned with the gun towards his desk. "Now, take a seat."

He sat down, ready for my next command. Just like an obedient dog. I liked that, as I have had some trouble in the past with other representatives. He knew his place.

"Now," I said, smiling. "As speaker for the Emperor, I am here to tell you we have a wonderful proposition for you and your planet."

"I will never side with the Empire. I am loyal to the Second Republic and the Second Republic alone. I would never be aligned with such filth as you," he snarled. It surprised me he would say such things, especially since he was on this god-forsaken rock.

"It's interesting you say that since the Republic is on the verge of declaring war with you, bombing a few of your key cities."

I watched as he gasped. It was always the same thing with these types of dramatic realizations, how a politician responded when they were betrayed by the government they swore fealty to, especially when I was sent to kill them by the Emperor himself.

"What? That is impossible, I swore my allegiance with them. Why would they do such a thing?"

"Simple. Your Chancellor decided to pick on you, to make sure his military weapons won't be taken from him. He's a dumbass, yes, but I used to work for him. What I say is true, I've seen the plans myself."

The Representative was silent, as if thinking it over. He never believed his so-called Chancellor would betray him like this. It was hard to explain, as part of it had to do with the future, with Wes having his wife die before his eyes on this planet, knowing it was the first to fall to the Empire. Well, history would repeat itself, Wes being the catalyst. And it all would end with more chaos and more destruction.

Who was the one with blood on their hands now, brother?

Allumas let out a brief sigh, as if he understood where that left him in all this mess. "If what you say is true, I need to think of my people."

"It is true."

He took a deep breath and looked out the window. "I have always wanted to help my people, that is why I became the Representative of this planet. The Senators are appointed by those on Valle, but not the people of the planet. They don't understand what it's like to be here. They don't see how much we suffer."

I stayed silent as I listened. I knew of the poverty this planet had to suffer through. Though I hadn't seen them myself, I could relate my harsh experience from the Kamps to this planet's hardships. I understood how one could only endure for so long and not be able to do anything about it.

"Since Chancellor Atkins has come to power, he has done nothing but cause turmoil to not only this planet, but many others like ours. He doesn't take the time to get to know his people, like the Chancellors used to. Our economy has been disrupted, causing many to go unemployed and living on the streets, which is difficult in this god-forsaken place." Allumas turned to me, his aging eyes appearing desperate. "Can you promise me that my people will be safe if we form an allegiance with the Pandronan Empire? Can you promise me that?"

So even this far before the alliance was supposed to happen, the Representative was having second thoughts about the Republic. That was good for me to hear, because that meant he would hear me out, would understand that this was the only way to keep his people safe. The Empire was the only way that he and his people could survive.

"I can promise that Emperor Joss will do everything in his power to make sure you are safe from the Republic. He will also do his best to restore the economy of this planet and in exchange you must promise your loyalty to us. If you do anything to break that promise, I can swear that this planet will suffer more than you could ever imagine."

The door opened, and Dan appeared out of nowhere. He closed the door behind him and locked it. He didn't say a word as he stepped beside me. Allumas studied him, but realized that he was with me. If he tried to back out now, there was no way he would get past us.

Not to mention that no one would come help him.

"Was it only you two that snuck in?" Allumas asked.

I nodded. "Yes."

He laughed. "Only two, huh? That shows me how powerful the Empire really is."

Allumas bit his thumb, thinking. It was something he didn't let the public see—showing his uncertainty was never good for a politician. I didn't care, from what I learned they were never certain about their actions. The only thing they were certain about was that if they screwed up, then they would send me to kill them.

"Fine. I will do it," he said. "I promise my loyalty to the Empire. I will send my men in my place to talk to your Emperor shortly and ban the senators of the Republic from ever stepping foot on this planet again. We are on your side of this war now."

"Thank you. We will await your appointed visit. We shall send you access codes to arrive to Anosira as soon as possible." I put the gun away and clapped my hands together. "Now, could you be ever so nice and call off your men? I don't want to be shot at when I step out of this office."

"Of course." He pushed a button on the table. "Johnson. Yeah, it's all clear. Just a misunderstanding. Seems they lost their passes and had to come in the back way. Call off the soldiers."

Dan held out his hand to Allumas. "Good to know that you have some sense in this universe. We will make sure this planet is safe, I guarantee it."

Allumas shook his hand. "Yeah, yeah. Leave here before I change my mind."

And with that, we left Representative Allumas alone in his office.

"Well that went easier than expected." I folded my arms behind my head, smiling in triumph as we walked through the corridors. "And I didn't have to even hurt him to make a point."

"Do you believe that violence is the only solution to getting a person to change their mind?" Dan asked as we walked out of the Capitol Building. People stared at us, but they did nothing to stop us. And why would they? Their Representative told them not to.

I shrugged, kind of surprised that Dan would ask such a question. He was the one who could beat me in a fight, yet he questioned my tactics. "No, but it's definitely the fastest and easiest. Besides, does the person who I haven't seen get beaten in a fight have an alternative way of persuading someone to their side?"

"That I do. Maybe something we can go over when we get back to Anosira, as part of your training."

I laughed. Now he was trying to be the good guy here.

After everything I had seen him be able to do, I knew no 'good' guy could ever come up with such things. There was a darker side to him than he was letting on, and I would figure out what that was. "We shall see. But for now, I will stick to my method." I took a deep breath, the crisp air entering my lungs. Felt like breathing in ice. I hated it here, I hated every time I got sent to this miserable planet for a mission. "Man it's cold. Would you mind getting me some coffee?"

He stared at me, narrowing his eyes. "You want me to get you coffee? Why don't you just come along? If you're so cold, then wouldn't you want to go inside the cafe?"

"Want to look around for a moment, breath in some fresh air. I will be right outside, waiting. Don't worry about that." I smiled. Yeah, it was a lie and he could see right through it. But Dan was nice, he would just give in to see what I would do. Maybe nice wasn't the right word, but curious.

"You aren't coming off as being honest, Myra," he sighed. "And I have no idea what you could be planning here."

"I told you, I am always honest. I just need some fresh air. Nothing to be suspicious about. Can't a girl ask a gentleman to get her some coffee? Now hurry before I get too cold to move."

He frowned, but gave in and went inside the cafe. As quickly as I could, I ran around the corner, searching for the exact brick Violet had told me to look for. I don't know if you ever have had to look for a certain brick before, but it was hard. They all looked the same, except the one I was looking for had something only I could decipher. Something only I could recognize.

Sanshlian letters.

To everyone else that passed by, it probably looked like chicken scratch. Because, well, it did look like chicken scratch. I also doubted people around here were that observant, as they tried to get from one location to the next before their body froze solid. Didn't blame them, really. I wished I was inside the cafe getting the coffee myself. But this was more important than keeping warm. This might be my only chance at getting home.

Once I spotted the brick with the lettering on it, I took my knife and carved it out of the building. I read the Sanshlian. It simply said Myra. I smiled, as that was all it needed to say for me to find it.

As Violet had said, it was hollow. I rattled it to find that it had something in it. Throwing it to the ground, the brick shattered, and a small clear gem was inside. I picked it up and examined it.

"So," I whispered to myself. "This what the fuss is all about? Shouldn't be surprised. Looks are deceiving. It's probably worth more than the entire universe's riches."

I pocketed the gem carefully with my pocket watch and hurried back to where I told Dan I would be waiting. Just as I stopped, he came out of the cafe.

"Where did you go?" Dan asked as he handed me to coffee.

I took a sip. "Didn't go anywhere. Just stayed here."

He raised an eyebrow. "Find that a little hard to believe."

Shrugging, I started forward towards the train station. "If you didn't trust me, you shouldn't have left me alone. Now, we should head back to Anosira, Joss will have another mission for us already. Speaking of which, you promised when we got back you would help me train on how to use my *special* powers. I would like to get that started, wouldn't you?"

He frowned, knowing I wouldn't tell him the truth about what I did. Did he let me go to see if I would tell him? He was a fool for sure to think I would tell him the truth. He should have known better by now. "Yeah, I guess. Nice change of subject."

I smiled. "You said I needed to work on changing a person's mind without violence."

He shook his head, a hint of a grin appearing on his face. He definitely enjoyed talking to me. "Whatever, let's just get out of here. The cold is getting to me."

Nodding, I agreed. "That's for sure."

We got on the train and started heading towards the port. I watched as we left the city, the snowy white covering everything around us. It looked like we were heading towards a snow storm and I wondered how it would affect the train. I doubted it would do anything, as Ttkas built everything to combat snow. I doubted we would even feel a shake of the car.

I breathed in and listened to the train itself. It seemed okay. Aging, I could tell. This train had seen so many travelers over the years, I could feel its weariness. It was strange to feel such things from an inanimate object, but I was getting used to it and enjoyed the connection. I felt I could link with something, even though it wasn't living in the sense that we knew life.

"You seem at peace while traveling. Most people are tense, but you seem at home while you are moving," Dan commented. I glanced over at him. He seemed cheerful now, not bringing up my disappearance when he got the coffee.

I stretched in my seat and leaned back. "I'm just used to traveling. I don't enjoy staying in one spot, too used to people after me. Staying means getting caught. So yeah, when I'm moving it means I'm safer."

We entered the tunnel, and the lights trickled on. Everyone around us went on with their business, waiting until they got to the port so they could leave this god-awful planet. I agreed with them, but being impatient wasn't worth my time. One could only go as fast as their choices allowed.

"What about you, where do you feel most at home?" I asked, trying to kill the time. Wasn't something I was used to doing, talking to another person, other than Lance that is.

He shrugged. "I haven't found a place to call home. I used to think home was where your loved one was, if you were with them, then anywhere could be home." Dan sighed. "But I was betrayed and now am alone, so I guess I never knew what home was. Maybe I will someday."

I nodded. "I think I understand."

"Jack?"

Frowning, I turned back to look outside, which was pitch black since it was a tunnel. "Still none of your business."

He laughed. "Sometimes you open up, and other times it's like hitting a brick wall. You need to work on your consistency."

"Yeah, well, you need to work on keeping your nose out of other people's business."

Dan went quiet, and I kept staring out at nothing. Time went by when the train came out of the tunnel. I could feel it before it happened, as the train was screaming out to me. Something bad was about to happen.

And suddenly the train stopped.

I jumped up, ready for anything, as did Dan. Everyone around us looked confused, frightened even. I glanced outside to find a group of five individual snow-cycles approaching. Someone was attacking the train. I almost laughed. This was the wrong train to mess with.

"Bandits?" Dan asked as he too looked out the window. "Well, this will get interesting."

I nodded. "Yes, it will." I pulled out my Class Two gun and raised it in the air so that all the other passengers would listen. "Listen up, there are bandits coming straight for the train. If you want to live, listen to what I have to say. None of you move, do you hear me? Crouch down in your seat and wait for this to be over."

There was always one that doesn't obey. He stood up. "I'm a Republic officer, I can help."

I aimed my gun straight at him. "No you can't. Sit

down. Now!"

It took him a minute, as if the gun pointed at him still made him think about what he should do next, like a deer in headlights. Such a joke of an officer. I turned to Dan.

"So what's the plan?" I asked.

"Plan?" he whispered. "I thought you would have come up with one by now."

"I have, but I didn't want to leave you out of all the work."

He smiled. "I am at your disposal on this mission. It's all up to you."

"Well then, if that's the case, here's the plan."

Chapter 13

Dan agreed to the plan I made in a jiffy, which was most of the plans I did, and I rushed forward to the other cars, shouting for all the people to get down. I didn't want to deal with shooting them if they got in my way. That wouldn't help the Representative trust the Empire. Stupid orders, always getting in my way, not to mention the paperwork that would have been involved. I hated paperwork.

There had to be someone on the inside, a person on the train connected to the bandits. That's how it always was —that way they could alert them of their location and where all the valuables were, which car to attack, etc. I just needed to figure out who it was. It would be obvious: the only person who wasn't scared. Then again, I was waving a gun around. Everyone should be scared in that respect. But they would try their hardest to fit in, so any disturbance that wasn't part of the plan then they wouldn't know how to react to it.

Meanwhile, Dan hid in the shadows, having my back and monitoring everything that was going on. He was the one to make sure I didn't get shot or stabbed, which was unlikely since I was a capable fighter. He would also survey those who were approaching the train, seeing if he could tell where the inside person could be, but I had a feeling the moment they approached, the person would join them. It was hard to tell sometimes, though, as many of these bandits had no brain or skill to go against people like us. People skilled in fighting and combat and used to putting themselves in dangerous situations all the time.

I got all the cars to keep quiet and still before the bandits got on the train. Damn automatic trains like this. No one steered the thing, but I had a feeling the authorities had been called. It would take them a good while before they showed up, being out in the mountains just outside the tunnel.

Which our bandits counted on.

When the first bandit stepped foot on the train, I opened fire. No reason to wait it out. It was all or nothing at this point. I just wanted to get leave the planet. This was just a waste of my time. Even if I got shot, I would still be fine. So unless they were an excellent aim, which I doubted, and shot me in the head, then everything would be okay.

First man was done, the bullet hitting him straight in the head. I was still a splendid shot. As he fell off the train onto the snow, the white innocence now tainted with red yet again, I wondered why he joined the bandits and robbed trains. He probably had a family to support or something. Didn't matter to me, as it didn't matter that everyone on this train also was supporting someone. Well, other than Dan and I.

The other four opened fire on me, and I shielded myself around a wall. Peering around, I shot another straight in the head. He didn't stand a chance.

Three to go.

There was more loud shooting, as if they thought they could shoot through solid metal. It was just a waste of ammo. I was always taught to save the ammo, only to shoot when I knew I had a kill shot, unless I just wanted to wound the person. That was pretty rare.

I shot two more times around the corner and two more men went down. All that was left was one.

"I—I surrender!" The last man yelled out. I let out a brief laugh.

"Not falling for that one!" I called out.

"I'm being serious, look." I heard him drop his gun. "I'm not armed, now please! I have a family that needs me."

I never understood that logic, for a criminal to get me to feel sorry for them because they had a family to feed. Did they not realize the people they were about to attack also had a family? They were showing no compassion to them, so why would I ever feel bad for their situation? "Should have thought about that before you attacked this train. The Empire doesn't allow criminals!"

He was silent for a moment. "The Empire?"

I forgot that the Empire didn't have control yet. It was just something that I was used to saying before I sent a bullet into my enemy. I guess it didn't matter now. I stepped out from behind the wall. He was unarmed. "Yes. Now." I raised my gun. "Goodbye."

The sound of a gun resonated through the car. The only problem was that it wasn't mine. Felt like my heart skilled a beat. I gulped as I turned around to find a man collapse behind me. Dan stood there, gun raised, smiling.

"Watching your back."

I nodded, looking at the man he just killed. "The insider?"

"Yup." He shot the gun again, at the man I was just about to kill. He hit the ground. "All done. Shall we wait for the authorities?"

He killed with such ease. It was creepy, as it must have been what I looked like when I killed a person. No remorse, just as if he was picking a weed in a garden. After he had told me there was another way to win a situation without violence, I found it strange he was so quick to kill.

I nodded. "Yeah, probably a good idea. It will help the Representative see that we will keep his people safe. Gonna delay us from leaving by a few hours though."

"Yeah, I was afraid of that," he rubbed the red scruff that was appearing on his face. It had been a while since he shaved.

I looked down at the bandits. They were all young, for bandits I mean. None could be older than twenty-five.

"Probably should have left one alive, so he could tell the tale of us killing his friends. Let fear spread across the criminal community."

Dan shrugged. "I think they will still get the message. Not like any others have been slaughtered like this. The Representative will let the planet know the Empire is now protecting them. It will go just as we want it to. Shall we alert the cars that all is safe now?"

I nodded. "Yeah, let's."

As I figured, it took a good few hours before we could leave the planet. The authorities wanted to talk to us, then they wanted to check with everyone on board, and then some paperwork. Stupid paperwork, it always got confusing since I didn't exist.

There was a video camera on the train, so what we said was verified. I think the Representative got word of what we had done and got everything to move by faster. I was thankful for that, as normally when the Empire ruled all the planets, I could just slip in and out of a situation a lot quicker, not having to worry about all the paperwork. I left that for someone else to deal with. Like Tom or the others. They always loved that.

It would be a good couple of days before we got to Anosira, so Dan and I got the chance to train in combat once again. On the nice hard metal floor.

Yay.

I hoped that he would give me a break, but no. I was wrong. We trained the moment we stepped on the ship and would until we got off. And then more training when we got back, but at least that would be for my powers. Then I could feel even more powerful. I wouldn't feel as weak as Dan made me feel.

Then I could defeat Nygard.

At least I felt I could release my frustrations while fighting. I could let out the anger I had for not knowing how to use my powers yet, some stupid guy almost shooting me on the train, the fact I had to lie to Jack again and again. I couldn't wait until this was all over, I couldn't wait until I could tell Joss to screw himself, that I was bringing forth peace in the galaxy and he could do nothing about it. Though, then again, I would have to say I finished destroying Nygard once and for all. I couldn't say it prematurely, or I would be the one that was screwed.

When I got on the ship, I hid the gem in my quarters, in a pair of one of my extra boots I brought. I figured it would be the best place to put it, not that Dan would go searching for it since he knew nothing about it. He knew I had disappeared, but he never knew it was to retrieve something. If it came up with Joss, I could put in my mind that I was there, that I hadn't run off. At least I learned that from my mother.

After a couple of hours of training, I retired to my quarters and pulled out the gem. It didn't seem like anything special and I had no idea how it would help me find Sanshli again.

"So you found it?" My mother appeared in the mirror across from my bed.

I nodded. "That I did. Now what I do?"

"*Wait until the time is right, when the light of darkness shines once again. Then you will be able to find Sanshli.*"

I let out a moan and collapsed on my bed. "Another freaking riddle? You have got to be kidding me? Why can't this ever be easy, why can't it be just, here's Sanshli, good luck in destroying Nygard?"

"*Because you need to make sure all the people from the future are on Sanshli to reverse this.*"

I jumped up. "What? You never said that! How am I supposed to even accomplish that?"

"*You will find a way. The clue will help you understand.*"

"I'm sick of this! Why can't you tell me?

"*Because there is more to all of this than you understand.*"

I rubbed my face. "Then tell me! How am I going to defeat him? I thought you were supposed to help me, but you won't even train me besides shielding my mind. Why can't you just give me all the information?"

"*That's just the way it is. Learn to live with it.*"

I thought about saying something back, but there was no use. She doesn't like my snarky attitude. I wanted to say I had lived through such horrible things growing up, that she just dumped me on a backwater planet to be captured and forced to take medication that would make me into a fighter I had to spit out every day. Then there was the painful trauma of being forced to fight and kill children the same age as me that I trained with and formed friendships with. Then, after that, I was taken out by the Emperor to become his servant, a killer, an assassin. I had gone through enough hardships that I just wanted it all to be over.

Was it too much to ask to live a normal life? Not be made to kill others, to have to fulfill a prophecy, to not be tortured like this?

But that wouldn't happen. That would never happen, I was destined for hardship, never being able to enjoy the things I wanted to. I didn't even know what I enjoyed. To be honest, everything I have done has been part of a mission. Life was just one mission after another.

"Okay," I sighed. "I will figure it out, I always do."

"That's my girl."

I grumbled under my breath. "I got to get some rest. Dan has been over working me lately, training me to become a better fighter."

I thought she would fade away, but she looked at me. *"Dan? Who's Dan?"*

"He's just one of the Emperor's lackeys. Nice guy, I guess, but one scary fighter. I can't even beat him in hand-to-hand combat."

Violent was silent for a moment. *"Just promise me you will be careful. And don't forget to shield your mind. You never know who can read your mind."*

"I know, I know."

"Listen to me, Myra. Promise me you won't let your thoughts slip, that you will keep your mind protected."

"I will," I whispered. "I promise."

"Then sweet dreams, my love." And with that, she disappeared.

It was odd, she never had such a reaction like this before. Dan was a nice guy, I wondered why she was so suspicious about him. Though, then again, she was suspicious about Lance, until I explained to her he was just obsessed with me. I guess after everything that has happened, she has trust issues. Although, so do I, yet something about Dan felt familiar, felt like I could believe in all that he says. It could just be curiosity, as I wanted to be strong like him. Whatever it was, I would figure it out. I always did.

I pulled the covers over myself and listened to the ticking pocket watch until I fell asleep.

Chapter 14

We arrived at Anosira just as planned. No space pirates stopping us, or Republic criminals, thank goodness. I didn't want to deal with that kind of paperwork again. It was a hassle.

I was surprised that nothing happened, because let's be honest, I was having a stroke of terrible luck. It felt too easy, just traveling back and forth between two planets. I felt like something was missing—that there should be an attack or something going horribly wrong.

Dan didn't manage to break my bones this time either. I was also thankful for that. It was like a routine traveling with him: sleep, eat, check systems on the ship, then train, eat, train, and sleep again. We switched off sleeping times, so someone was always awake. He slept right after I did, as I ate and checked systems. We got into the groove of things just as we arrived to Anosira, which meant I would have to shift my schedule once again. That was one problem with traveling: having to change one's routine, especially meals and sleep. After a while, though, I got the hang of it. I never enjoyed sticking to one routine too long anyway. Made life seem boring.

We reported straight to Joss, as he wanted to know how everything went. We reported from the planet when the Representative agreed to siding with the Empire; it was on the news and everything. He had already told the senators to go back to Valle and tell Wes that his loyalty and the planet's loyalty were to the Empire. He also thanked us for saving a train full of his people, though he made it sound more like there were quite a few Imperial troops on the train when it had just been the two of us. That was a good thing, though, as Dan and I weren't your typical Imperial soldiers.

I had a feeling that the Republic would attack soon, and that the senate was freaking out. Wes would have his wish in attacking Ttkas, though he wouldn't have the element of surprise on his side this time, not to mention all the Imperial forces that were now heading that way. Whatever, that was someone else's job, not mine.

No, mine was much more complicated.

Anyhow, Joss wanted to know the details of what happened on Ttkas. He wanted to hear an account of how I did from Dan, if I was any trouble. I wasn't, I swore, but I wondered if Dan would mention that I had disappeared for a brief amount of time. Even if he didn't,

Neil may read his mind and see that had happened. Hopefully he trusted Dan enough to not resort to such measures, but I doubted it.

The gem I had already taken to my room on Anosira and hid in another pair of boots. I had no idea where to put it otherwise. Joss would look everywhere if he found out about its existence, and search me. So maybe he wouldn't think I would be stupid enough to put it in my spare boots.

Dan and I met up again and arrived to Joss' office in the palace. Joss clapped as we walked in. I looked at him, confused. Clapping at us was not something I would have expected. He even looked happy, which was something I hadn't seen in a very long time. As for why, I did not know.

"Very, very good defeating those bandits. It forced the Representative to side with us, knowing we will keep his people safe. Nice work," Joss said.

"Oh, yeah, that," I mumbled. So it wasn't the mission, it was about the train. I should have figured. "That was not planned."

"It wasn't?" Joss smiled as he stood up. I glared at him. He had sent those men to our train so we would deal with them and show the Representative what we were capable of. It was a set up, I had been used yet again.

Joss went on. "Anyway, I have sent him the codes to land on Anosira, he should send men soon. I have already sent Imperial officers in his direction to take over all the armed forces and weapon manufacturers. Wesley won't know what hit him."

"Which means the Republic will retaliate soon. We will need to prepare for that," Dan said. I agreed, but I wasn't one to get ready for a war like this. I was the one behind the scenes usually, assassinating those who came in the way of the Empire. I wondered if that would be my next task, after learning my powers of course.

"Yes, I am working on that," Joss explained. I was glad I wasn't in his shoes at this moment. I would have to deal with all the stuff that he had to plan to keep his power over other planets. Though, I guess by now he was used to it. "Some of the other generals will be stationed at the planet, ones that aren't from the future, ready to attack at a moment's notice. As for you two, I want you to train Myra in using her powers. She will be vital to us once that is done. So in the meantime, you two are stuck on the planet."

"If you wanted me to train, then why did you send us to Ttkas?" I asked. "Wouldn't it have been easier to just send someone else?"

"You know as well as I that we wouldn't have been able to deal with the planned attack by the Republic if you didn't persuade the Representative to join us. Besides," his glance shifted to Dan. "I wanted Dan to tell me how you behaved, if you seemed at all out of the ordinary."

Dan was quick to answer. "She did nothing, Emperor. She did as she was told. She is quite good at her job, actually. It surprised me."

It amazed me that Dan didn't tell him about my

disappearance, but I hid those thoughts from my mind. I had no idea if Joss was reading my mind or not. Or if he was reading Dan's and, if so, whether he would say anything.

I smiled. "See, nothing to worry about."

Joss didn't seem too persuaded by what I said. "Fine, but if I catch you doing anything out of the ordinary, Myra, I swear I will make you wish you were never born."

"Oh, believe me, I know." Not to mention I already wished I was never born. I didn't know what Joss could do that would be any worse than the things I had been through, though I didn't doubt he could be creative.

Joss sighed. "Very well, you are dismissed Myra. Dan, I still need to talk to you."

Dan nodded, and I turned and walked out of the office. I didn't want to deal with Joss more than I needed and was glad I could leave. I could feel my anger climbing every time I saw him and it was getting harder to hide.

Speaking of hiding, as I stepped out of the office, I spotted Tim in the distance.

"Shit," I whispered. I had nowhere to go without passing him, and I didn't want him to talk to me. I didn't want to lie to him again. It was too hard.

Then suddenly, General Logan appeared before me. I didn't want to do it, I knew I would never hear the end of it, but I knew it was the only way to get Tim to stop pursuing me.

So I quickly grabbed Logan and shoved him against

the wall.

His green eyes widened. "What the f—"

Before he could finish that thought, I pressed my lips against his. I couldn't tell by his body if he was resistant or persuaded by the fact I was kissing him. He kind of just stood there, taking it and not caring, that or plotting his revenge against me. Most likely the latter if I knew Logan like I did. I turned a bit to see if Tim saw us. He did, his face appearing heartbroken. He turned around and started for the opposite direction to get away from both of us.

I stopped kissing Logan and let him go. He frowned as he looked at me. I didn't know what to say, so I just stood there, silent, waiting for him to speak.

He sighed. "Was that necessary?"

I wiped my lips with the back of my glove. "What?"

He looked like he was about to punch me, but took a deep breath, letting it all go. "Is that what you do every time you are trying to avoid someone? If I recall, you kissed Thomas on Ttkas after you betrayed the Empire."

I shrugged, wanting to forget about kissing Thomas. It was one of my lowest points in my life. "Depends. It worked, didn't it?"

Rolling his eyes. "Just don't do it again. You are lucky I didn't kill you."

"Would like to see you try, Pete. Or it's Logan now, isn't it?"

"That it is. Now leave me be. Unlike some people, I have work to be done."

"I have work to do too!" I called after him as he

walked off. I let out a brief sigh as I headed towards the training room, a little excited. It was my first day learning to use my powers after all.

Also, I didn't realize before now that Logan was an excellent kisser, even if he wasn't trying. He tasted like citrus.

Dan didn't take too long speaking with Joss in private and met me in the training center. There were a few other people there, and I started practicing on the bags before Dan came. It was always my "go to" item for training, as I did a lot of hand-to-hand combat. It was worth my time to build on my strengths.

When Dan came in, he motioned me to leave the training room. "Come, we are going outside to train."

"Really?" I asked as I hurried after him. "I haven't done that before. I usually train inside. Never occurred to me until now that I never went outside much. Except to run, of course. I guess it had to do with me wanting to stay close to the Emperor in case he needed me for something. That, and I scared people that I wasn't supposed to out in the open."

Dan laughed. "I could see that. But where we are going you don't have to worry about others seeing you. We will be secluded for a while."

I asked no more questions, knowing that it would all be revealed to me, and learning anything ahead of time wouldn't give me any advantage. I was to train my powers at last, and there was no way I knew how that would happen.

When I thought about it, it was probably a smart idea to go somewhere secluded. If we were in the training room and something went wrong, like terribly wrong, I could hurt the Capitol Building, and Joss would be pissed if I did that. And we didn't want any others seeing us, as it wasn't normal for someone to manipulate elements, or whatever we would do. I was an illusionist, and I knew it wouldn't be so simple as what David and the others had to learn. No, what I had to do was more complicated, it wasn't taking something and making it work for me. It was creating something completely different.

At least, that's what I heard. I didn't know.

We grabbed a Class Two hovercraft, and Dan piloted it to where he wanted to train. I could barely sit still, excited that I would start to learn what I was capable of. Violet wouldn't teach me such things, warned me that my powers were like a curse, but I didn't care. I saw them as something I could wield to defend myself, something I could use to be as powerful as I wanted, to not have to worry about others trying to hurt me. I would always have the advantage. No one would dare go against me.

I watched out the window as we left the city and went into the outskirts. It was so secluded here, so pristine. There was so much nature that appeared untouched by human hands, as many wanted to keep it that way. It was almost like Garvner but far more advanced. I hadn't been back to my home world since before we came back in time. I couldn't even imagine what it would be like in the time we were at.

Oh, right. It would be the same.

Dan flew us to a small little island off the coast and landed. There was nothing here except jungle and sand. Were we going to train here? It was strange. I thought we would at least be in some abandoned building.

"Now," Dan said as he unbuckled himself. "Let's get started."

Chapter 15

"What are we doing way out here? Seems a little odd," I said as I looked around. There was nothing but sand, water, and jungle. I doubted there were any animals on the island, other than birds, but I had an irrational fear that an enormous cat would pounce on me. Stupid Brayen and him scaring me on Sanshli when we first arrived to the planet. He had been Violet's best friend and guarded the planet for thousands of years. I couldn't believe he had so much dedication. But I would never get the irrational fear that an animal would attack me out of my head, not to mention I still had nightmares every once in a while about such things happening. Though this time instead of warning me what would happen, it was just my fear of it all replaying again and again. I swore if I saw Brayen again, I would deck him.

"We will work on element manipulation." Dan sat down on a rock. It didn't look so comfortable, therefore I would prefer just to sit on the sand. It had been a while since I had lay down on the sand. The last time was with Jack.

Dan broke my train of thought. "Now, see the ocean over there? Make an orb out of the water and send it at me."

I raised an eyebrow. "Really? You want me to get you soaking wet?" I glanced over at the ocean. "And how? I have no idea how to do that."

"Just concentrate. Want it, think about how it would look, how it would feel in your mind. That is all you need to do."

"Psh, easy for you to say," I mumbled. He wasn't the one doing this, but I was told that he was the one who helped the others train. He must just be an excellent teacher or something, or pissed the others off enough that they mastered their element so they didn't have to deal with him any longer. I wasn't sure which it was, but if the others could master their powers, so could I.

It was strange for Lance, Wes, and Alan to master their powers so quickly. They just stumbled across them, Lance wanting some water and it came straight to him and splashed his face, which was hilarious might I add. Same for the others. For me, though, it never came like that. Was that because I was born with them? That I had neglected to think about them, so therefore they never showed up? I could heal and was extra strong—that came to me with no problems, but as for the other things that illusionists could do, I didn't know how to do any of that.

"Well, here goes nothing," I whispered as I raised my hand up. I knew in my mind that raising my hand would do nothing for it. I mean, it was all in my mind, not actual muscles or anything, but I just couldn't help it. It made me focus on the water, seeing my hand out like that. So I kept it out. I stood there for at least a minute.

I tried to think of how I felt in ships and around trees and buildings and such. I could feel how they worked, what they experienced as if they were living things. I wondered if it had to do with that connection, that I could try to connect with the water, feel it, and get it to do as I said. I concentrated on that, trying to understand the element of water.

Surprising enough I felt it, could think like it, could experience all that it offered. I imagined it forming into a ball just as I wanted it to, just as it needed to to prove to Dan that I was as powerful as my colleagues. That I was more powerful.

And…. Nothing.

I sighed. "It's not working Dan, I don't think—" I heard a gun cock. I turned a bit to find Dan with a Class Two pointed at me.

"Do it, or I'll shoot you in the leg." Dan didn't waver.

"What?" I exclaimed. He couldn't be serious. Was this what he did with the others? I doubted it, Thomas would have thrown a fit.

"You heard me. I will shoot you in the leg."

I stared at him, not sure if he was joking. He had that

calm look, almost as if he was a madman, but not quite. It was the same look he gave when he killed those two men.

The same look I give everyone.

"I'm waiting," he said.

Turning back at the task at hand, I kept trying to raise the water into a ball and hitting Dan with it. I thought about the water, I thought of how it was an element, how it was a part of this world and the universe. I thought of the cycles it possessed, the things it had done and seen.

But no matter how much I concentrated, nothing would happen.

I dropped my arm, letting out the breath I had been holding. "I can't, I just can't."

And he shot me. I felt the bullet hit me straight in my left leg. I went down, yelping in pain.

"You jackass! You shot me!" I exclaimed. I could believe it, I didn't think he would do it, that he would cause me this much pain because I couldn't control the water right away. "What kind of psycho trainer or you? Who does that? Did you shoot the others? Damn it, what the heck, Dan?" I was babbling. The person I had trusted this long had just shot me for failing. I wondered if Joss had ordered him to. Either way, I was pissed and Joss would hear all about it.

Dan stood up and came to where I was lying on the ground. "You heal fast. Don't worry about it."

I glared at him. I wanted to hit him, but not with some stupid ball of water. I wanted to hit him with a good-sized rock. I wanted to do it at this point.

Suddenly Dan caught something behind his head. I blinked, not sure what had just happened. He held out his hand to reveal a rock the size of a baseball.

Had I done that? It was how I imagined it and where I wanted to hit him. Somehow, with all the emotions flowing through me, I could muster enough power to make the rock almost hit him.

Dan smiled. "Now we are getting somewhere."

Dan took me back to the Capital, as I needed someone to take the damn bullet out of my leg. I was pissed at him, but also excited that I could move that rock. His method had worked, although I didn't know if he thought I would get the water to move before he shot me or if he figured the rock thing would happen first. I also wondered if he had shot anyone else to help them train, or if it was just me he used such unconventional techniques.

Probably just me. I was always so lucky like that, getting the psychotic person to train me and for them to think they could use any means necessary. Especially after they found out I could heal fast. Though, luckily for me, most of those trainers didn't last long.

A doctor took the bullet out and Joss had me released from the infirmary before they could ask questions about why the wound was already healing. I didn't want to explain it to them all, that I could heal fast. I didn't want to be a test subject, not again. Though I knew Joss wouldn't let them do anything to me, he didn't need that kind of stuff to deal with.

After they released me, I went straight to Joss' office, wanting to complain to him about what Dan had done, not that he would care. He would just think it was funny and then make me go back out to that island and tell Dan to shoot me again, even if I made a water orb hit him next time around.

"Joss, I have a bone to pick with you." I barged into his office as I usually did. To my surprise, Tim was in there talking to him. If I had known that, I wouldn't have come. I didn't want to see him, not right now. Not when I was already angry with life and everything. "Oh, sorry. I didn't realize there was someone else in here."

"Like you have ever cared," Joss commented. I gave him a look, though I knew it was true. Usually I did just barge into areas, even if he had Representatives with him. Though it was for good reasons, just like this one was. Dan had shot me for crying out loud.

"I was just leaving." Tim shoved past me, not making eye contact.

I watched as he closed the door behind him. It hurt a little that he didn't even care to look at me. I would explain it all later, I told myself, and then he would know the truth. I masked those thoughts from Joss.

"What was that about?" I asked as I turned my attention back to Joss.

"It was nothing of your concern. But interesting, in his mind I saw you kissing Logan." Joss had a bit of a smirk on his face when he said that, as if he found it amusing.

I rolled my eyes. "Oh, you know very well why I did that. I didn't want to talk to him again. If he saw me with someone else, I knew he would leave me alone."

Joss laughed. I hated how he thought all of this was almost like a comedy for him to enjoy. "Very well, I bet Logan was ecstatic you picked him."

"I think if I did it again, he would run me through with a sword. But that's not the point. I wanted to talk to you about Dan."

His lips turned into a slight smile. "Oh? What about him?"

"What about him? He shot me!" I exclaimed. Yup, this was how I thought he would react. Thinking it was all so funny. I wanted to shoot someone so bad or be sent on some mission where I could take it out on someone else.

Where was Thomas when I needed him?

"But it worked, didn't it? You were able to move that rock?" Joss asked as he straightened some papers on his desk.

I slammed my fist on the table. "That's not the point! He shot my leg!"

Joss gave me a look, making me realize I shouldn't have showed so much anger. He hated it when I did that. Then he shook his head. "Why does that matter? You heal fast, you will be fine by tomorrow morning. Just be lucky that he cared enough to just shoot you in the leg instead of the torso."

"How would that be worse?"

He shrugged. "Could have messed up, caused other complications. Anyway, you will return to your training tomorrow. And you better do as he says or you, well, will get shot again."

I shook my head. "That isn't fair and you know it."

"Life's hard, get over it. Would you rather I send you back to your brother? You think he will treat you any kinder? You have more freedom here than you ever did there. Be thankful that I don't have someone watching you at all times and that you are being able to use your powers."

"Why would you need someone to watch me, you are already reading my mind," I mumbled.

He stood up, his eyes dark as I remembered them once being. It was scary to think of all the times I had made him mad, where he couldn't just let me get away with something. The other generals didn't know what he was capable of, why I had feared him like I did. Why I never ran away.

"What was that?" he asked.

"Nothing, sir. It was nothing," I answered. He slapped my face, the burn on my cheek lingering on my face for a few moments. I rubbed my jaw.

"Message clear?"

I nodded. "Yes sir. Sorry sir."

"Now get back to work."

I bowed and headed towards my quarters where I could rest my leg before training tomorrow. I just prayed that I wouldn't get shot again.

Chapter 16

Sure enough, Dan took me to the same damn island to train me more. I was ready to get shot again, but when we stood on the beach, he changed his tactics.

Thank goodness.

"I promise not to shoot you today Myra, I'm sorry I used such drastic measures yesterday." He sounded remorseful about the fact he shot me, which was surprising since he had that wicked look on his face when he shot me the day before. There was no way someone could look like that and then feel remorse afterwards. It was an act which meant only one thing.

He was a superb actor. And I needed to be careful around him.

"Some reason I don't quite believe you, Dan," I said back. I waited for his instructions. I had learned how to control rock through his tactics yesterday. It seemed like he knew what he was doing in the long run, though I didn't quite agree nor knew what would happen from here on out.

He laughed. "Fair enough. But today I wanted you to focus on moving different elements. Like the rock. Can you do that again for me?"

I narrowed my eyes. It seemed too easy. "What's the catch?"

"There's no catch. Just want you to focus."

I did not believe him at all. There was always a catch in everything that happened with him. There was a catch in everything that surrounded me. So I couldn't help but to not trust him. Especially after he was so willing to shoot me, and those two men.

But I wouldn't know what that would be until I tried. Which—ironically—was how almost my entire life was. I never knew the outcome of anything, I just hoped for the best. Whether that was good or bad is still up for debate. I just knew that I was still alive, and that was all that mattered.

And how I got here was up for debate. Was it destiny or was it sheer rotten luck? No one could tell, or at least I hadn't come up with any explanation yet..

Taking a deep breath, I closed my eyes, focusing on the water in front of me. I wanted to control it, to become part of the water. I could feel it; I could see it in my mind, but that was it. I couldn't get it to listen to me, to obey my command like I needed it to.

The other problem was that the thought of controlling

water reminded me of Lance and how he splashed my face right before I tricked him into kissing me and knocking him out.

Maybe Logan was right, that was my 'go to' way to get out of something. It was just so easy and distracted men, and women, all too well. Especially Jack in a lot of cases, like when I was hiding something. He knew I used it to distract him, but he never seemed to mind.

It was also not the first time I had done that to Lance, as I had kissed him when we were trying to find Sanshli a year ago. I just hoped Lance wasn't mad at me. He knew that it was something I had to do to keep my sanity and not kill my brother, though that may be my task, eventually.

Well, not exactly. I needed everyone alive on Sanshli to reverse this mess. How I would do that, I did not know.

So I tried to focus on the task at hand and move the water into an orb. If Lance could do it, then so could I. There was no way I would let him out do me, let him defeat me like this. He had no one to train him, just stumbled across his powers. I couldn't be the odd one out.

I thought about how the water flowed, how it moved, manipulated by its surroundings, yet a powerful force all on its own. There was so much more going on with how the element worked, I was quite surprised. I tried to embrace it, feel it as if it flowed through me. Then I imagined myself as the water, as an orb in the sky.

I took a deep breath and opened my eyes. There, in front of me, was a large orb of water the size of a basketball. I smiled.

"You did it! Great job!" Dan exclaimed.

I focused on the water and watched it move and hit Dan straight on. His face was priceless, complete surprise as he was soaked. I laughed. It was worth it to see his face like that.

He wiped some water off his face. "I deserved that, yes."

Nodding, I agreed. "Yeah, you did. Now what's next?"

Dan got me to focus on other elements, just as like with water I had to manipulate air, fire, and vegetation. We already knew I could focus on rocks and I think he was still a little afraid that I would hit him in the head again. I wondered why.

I was feeling more powerful now, as if I could do anything. I no longer felt like the odd one out around the others from the future, around Logan or Joss. I could have the upper hand. And I was one step closer to defeating Nygard.

I still didn't understand why Violet didn't want to train me with this power if Nygard was out there. Wouldn't she want me to be powerful? Wouldn't she want me to defeat my father? It made little sense, why she would leave me weak like this. And I knew if I asked, she wouldn't answer me. It was always back and forth with her. Nothing was ever answered.

Not to mention I had to solve another riddle to find Sanshli.

What was with Sanshlians and riddles? Seriously, it

was annoying. Though what I didn't understand was the fact that my mother didn't know the answer to this one. Wasn't she the one who made these riddles up? So either she wasn't the one who did it or she was lying to me.

Honestly, I didn't know which one it was.

Dan and I headed back to the Capitol Building where he said I would practice more. I didn't understand why I couldn't just keep practicing on the island, but I decided not to bother. It wasn't like he would give me a straight answer, anyway. It didn't seem like anyone was giving me straight answers, ever. I learned to deal with it though, as I had all my life.

Following him to the training room, I found it empty. It had grown late now, and it didn't surprise me. It was almost dark out now, as it had taken some time for us to travel back.

"Wait here, I will be right back," Dan said as he hurried out the door. I rocked back and forth on my heels. I wondered what Dan was doing, a little curious, a little afraid. He had shot me after all, he was capable of anything. A couple moments later, he appeared with Logan. The moment he saw me, he rolled his eyes.

"What am I doing here?" he asked. "And why do you want me to work with her?"

"I need you to just stand still and when you need to, use your powers," Dan explained.

Logan sighed and stood still. "Just promise me she won't try and kiss me again."

Dan glanced over at me, a little confused. I shrugged. "I have no idea what he's talking about. Anyway, what do you want me to do?"

"I want you to focus on creating a wall of fire around Logan. Can you do that?" Dan asked.

I didn't think I could, but I didn't want Logan to know that. I was the last to master my powers, and I hated it when someone could defeat me like he could with them. He looked at me, waiting for something to happen. If I didn't do it, he would tell the others I had failed at something. I would never hear the end of it, as I never showed failure in anything to them.

Taking a deep breath, I focused on fire, wanting it to spread out and around Logan. At first there was nothing, but I kept concentrating, kept wanting it to appear. I couldn't show weakness, I couldn't let Dan down. Because, frankly, he might shoot me again.

And it appeared, just as I imagined it. I had done it.

Logan wasn't impressed. He just stood there for a moment and let out a brief sigh. A second later, he waved his hand, and a sheet of ice and fog appeared. The fire was gone; he had wiped it away with his powers.

Son of a bitch.

He turned to Dan, as if all of this had been troublesome. It was his typical demeanor so I shouldn't have taken it personally, though it was a little late for that.

"Can I go now?" he asked.

Dan nodded, and Logan left the training room. I wanted to run after him and punch him. I had made a beautiful firewall for him, and he destroyed it with his powers.

Which meant I was still weak. Which meant training all day was for nothing. And I had made a fool of myself in front of Logan. This day just couldn't get any worse.

I cursed myself for thinking that. Now it would get so much worse.

Dan clapped his hands together. "Well done, Myra. I think we can call this a day."

I couldn't believe what I was hearing. After all that, he was just going to give up for the day. I still wasn't powerful enough. I still wanted to do more. "But he cleared it away. He destroyed it."

"Yes, but you could create something much larger than what we were doing on the island. I had a feeling if you were around your colleagues, you might improve faster. As for him blocking it, that is something to work on tomorrow. You have to remember that others have powers as well, so you must work on strengthening them to defeat them. If your fire was strong enough, it could have withstood the ice. But you aren't there yet, they have had a year of training and you have had just two days. You will get there soon, I promise."

For some reason, Dan's little speech didn't lighten up my anger. I nodded and thanked him for the day. As quickly as I could, I headed to my quarters. I didn't want to deal with another person for the rest of the day.

But of course, that would never happen. There always had to be more complications, more things to irritate me.

Like the whole thing with Tim.

Tim was waiting for me outside my quarters. I took a deep breath and walked straight towards him.

"What do you want?" I asked. I sounded a little angrier than I wanted, but I was still irritated that Logan had bested me at powers that weren't even actually his. I was the only one here that was born a Sanshlian, except for Neil of course. It irritated me that it came so naturally to them, yet so hard for me.

Tim looked sad, his eyes round and sorrowful. I was glad he wasn't Jack from the future in appearance because I could never say no to those eyes. It was a little easier with him now looking like someone else. Just a little. "I just wanted to know the truth. I want to know if you are in a relationship with Logan."

Oh, the dilemma. Do I lie and say that I was, and have Logan try to kill me when he found out, as he would never go along with it, or do I say no and have to explain that I kissed Logan to make him go away? Neither choice was preferable over the other, and I was running out of time.

"We have had some relations, yes." That was all I could come up with. That way it sounded like we were together, but the relations we had was a hateful relationship full of resentment.

"So we are really over? After all this time? I can't believe that." Tim grabbed my wrist. "I will *never* believe that."

"Let me go," I said in an earnest tone. "I don't love you, I have only been using you for the Emperor. My loyalty is to him and him alone."

"You are telling me that this entire time, all the missions on Recar, they were never to see me? That you lied to me every time we were together? That you just wanted an 'in'?"

"Yes. I never loved you Jack, I was ordered to get close to you for information, for Recar's loyalty to the Empire. Now that is done, I have no use for you," I lied. I couldn't believe what I was saying. I couldn't believe I had to hurt him like this, after all this time.

He shook his head. "You are lying, you have to be."

I had to finish this, this had to be the last time I lied to him. "I'm sorry, but that's the truth. Now leave."

He stared at me for a moment longer, then turned and left without another word. I took a deep breath, knowing that was the point where he had given up on me.

I just didn't know if that was a good thing or a bad thing.

Chapter 17

I lay on my bed, exhausted, both physically and mentally. After everything that had happened today, I needed a drink. First, I had a long day of learning my powers, only to find out I was behind everyone else. Then on top of that I had just lost Jack forever, and I could bet that some others would pick on me when Logan told them I couldn't beat him with my powers. I had so much to do and yet so far to go. I wasn't used to that feeling; I was used to being the best.

But now it felt like I had to start all over.

At least now I had Dan to teach me things, instead of no one like earlier. I could trust that he would get me where I needed to be to defeat Nygard. Then this would all be over. I reached over to my boot and picked up the gem. It would be soon, I knew it deep down.

The gem glistened in the light. It was a beautiful emerald color, maybe it was an emerald, though I knew it was much more advanced than that. Somehow this little gem would tell me where Sanshli was, where the darkest light shone.

That made no sense, but it was Violet who said it. So it had to be true. As I thought this over, I heard my mother's voice.

"What are you thinking?" she asked.

I sighed as I put my arm over my eyes. "I'm just exhausted. I trained all day and then had to break my love's heart. It takes it out of one when that happens."

"I'm sorry sweetheart, but you know that it's for the best. That it's for the safety of the universe. Hopefully after it all ends, he will understand."

"Will I, or he, even be alive after all of this ends?" I asked. Violet didn't answer. I let out a brief laugh. "I didn't think so."

"It is unknown what will happen after you defeat Nygard, whether anyone will survive."

"That sounds reassuring."

"I'm just telling you I don't have all the answers."

I sat up. "Then what answers do you have, mother? What can you tell me so I can win? So I can end this, and the pain can go away? I'm just sick and tired of everything. I want this over with."

She shook her head in the reflection. *"I don't know, I'm sorry."*

I held up the gem. "You have no idea what the darkest light is?"

Violet paused. *"No, I don't."*

"Then how come I think you are lying to me? How come you have to lie to me?"

"It's just so much more complicated than you could ever imagine."

"Explain it to me so I can understand!"

Violet's face reddened. *"I can't. You aren't ready!"*

Just as I was about to reply, I heard a knock at the door and I put the gem in my pocket with my watch. My mother's appearance disappeared from the mirror and I took a deep breath, hoping it wasn't Tim again. I didn't want to face him, didn't think I could. "Come in."

It was Dan. Should have known. His face was bright as it always was, which I didn't understand how it could be at this late at night after training me all day. He was unique, I gave him that.

"What are you doing here?" I asked, not bothering to get up. I didn't feel like that, and formality had flown out the window once I told Tim off.

He sat across me in the chair, concern now apparent on his face. He must have gathered I was upset. Didn't surprise me, I wasn't hiding the fact I was pissed off at the moment. "I saw you and Tim just now…"

I sighed. I didn't need another person prying into my personal life. My mother was enough to deal with. "Not this again. I already told you it's none of your business. Can you just leave me alone? Why do you even care?"

"I just… want to make sure you are okay."

"You want to make sure I am okay? Then don't shoot me in the leg," I retorted. He made no sense. What kind of person will shoot another person and then care to ask them about their personal life? A psychotic one, that's what. Though, other than how he deals with death, he didn't seem that psychotic, but I had the feeling that's what most people said about him. It was why Joss let him stay. He was as crazy as the rest of us.

"If you love him, talk to him, that's all I'm saying. And I would cover for you if Joss found out."

I raised my eyebrow. "What do you mean? How could you cover for me? Joss can read minds."

"I know that you are hiding your thoughts from Joss. It's something an illusionist can do. So the only person he would know it from is Tim. If Joss thinks something is going on, I can tell him that Tim is making it up. It was something that he wanted, not something that happened."

I stared at him, unable to believe what I was hearing. How could he know that? How could he know that and not let Joss know about it? "You know I can block my mind and haven't told Joss?"

He nodded. "Yes."

"Why?"

"Because he will hurt you and I can't bear to think of what he would do should he discover the truth."

I frowned. He cared about my well-being. That was weird to think about. "But you shot me."

"Yes, I did. But did it hurt you? How Joss would hurt you if he found out you loved Jack? That you would do anything to get him back?" he asked.

I didn't say a word. Yeah, it hurt, but it was a pain I

could get over. The things that Joss could do to me, however, were far worse than just getting shot in the leg. I knew that from experience. I knew that after all the times I tried to assassinate him.

I let out a sigh. "Fine. But I don't think I will go talk to Tim. There is no point, Joss will find out and I will be screwed. He can still read Tim's mind. So although you could help me out, I doubt we could get around that."

"That is up to you, I'm just letting you know that if you do talk to him, for real, I have your back."

"Thanks." And that was the only times I had ever thanked someone other than Jack. It was because I never relied on someone enough, that and every time I did I got stabbed in the back. So for him to do this for me seemed a little suspicious. There had to be more to it than his concern for me.

Dan nodded and left me there by myself in my room. He had a point, though. If I could block all the thoughts from Joss, Dan could talk Joss down from killing me. He wouldn't have complete proof. It could just appear as something Tim wished, which he did.

So did that mean I could go back to Jack without Joss knowing?

I bit my lip. I yearned to be in Jack's arms, to feel his warmth. It was the only thing I enjoyed in my life and I didn't think I could go on knowing that had been taken away from me.

So I did it. So I got up and left my quarters to talk to Tim. To talk to Jack.

* * *

I knocked on Tim's door, my heart racing in my chest. I didn't know if this would be an enormous mistake—if I should turn away now or if I should lie and say I was there for another reason. But I had already decided: I would tell him the truth.

That I love him and would forever love him.

It was as simple as that, right? To tell someone you loved them? Maybe not after what I had said before, but if Dan was right, if I could hide those thoughts, would Joss find out? Could Dan keep me safe? I sure hoped so, otherwise I was screwed.

Beyond screwed, as Joss clarified that if I screwed up, I would regret the day I was born. But the joke was on him, I already regretted that day.

The door slid open. Tim stood there, rubbing his face. He must have already fallen asleep since we talked, though it had been over an hour. I guess he wasn't as distraught as I had been, wanting to drink my sorrows away. Maybe he had some alcohol in his quarters.

`He was shirtless, all he had on were just his pajama bottoms. Damn, he was sexy. I thumbed the gem in my pocket, trying to calm myself down. I couldn't stand seeing him like this, I wanted to do things I wasn't proud of.

"What do you want?" he asked. He didn't seem pleased to see me, though I understood why. I had just broken his heart. I wouldn't be surprised if he slammed the door in my face. I would have to.

"I came here to explain what was going on," I whispered. I hoped no one could hear us, that everyone else was asleep. "Or at least, what I can."

"What is there to explain? Your relationship with Logan is more than you want to admit. And your loyalty is to the Emperor and the Emperor alone. I get it."

I shook my head. That was far from the truth. It had all been a lie because of Joss. I didn't want it to keep going, I didn't want to keep lying to the one person who cared. "No, I did it to make you leave. I thought it would work, but I felt horrible about it. In order to regain Neil's trust back I had to leave you Jack, I couldn't do it. I can't do it." I pulled him closer and kissed him.

I must have taken him by surprise because at first he just stood there for a moment, then I could feel his passion match mine. We hadn't been able to touch like this, to be this connected. All that had built up and I could feel it as I pressed my lips against his.

He pulled me inside his quarters, letting the door slide closed behind me, his warm flesh against mine. He was so warm, like a furnace. Even after everything, I wanted him to keep me close—to keep the fire inside my cold heart alive.

I shoved him down on his bed, pulling my tank off in the process. Joss would kill me, I knew that. But it was worth it as I looked down at his blue eyes. They watched me and took in everything about me. He brushed his fingers against my skin and I let out a brief sigh.

"I knew you loved me Arcadia. I knew it had to have been some kind of act," he whispered as he pulled me closer and kissed me.

I pulled back my head. "What did you just call me?"

"Arcadia, or I guess Myra now."

I stared at him. Jack never called me Arcadia unless he was trying to make me listen to him. Only when he got mad at me, but this definitely was not one of those times.

Then it hit me. This man wasn't Jack. He never was. They had lied to me, they all tricked me just to see what I would do.

Which meant he could only be one person. The one person I hadn't seen the entire time I was here. The person who was supposedly away on a mission. Apparently, this was his mission.

"You son of a bitch! Thomas you son of a bitch!" I jumped off of him and grabbed my shirt and put it back on. I was on the verge of wanting to kill him, or at least beat him until near death. Then I would let him heal and do it all over again.

Tim, who apparently was Thomas, leaned forward with a sly smile. "What gave me away? Does he have some kind of nickname for you in bed?"

I scowled at him. "I'm going to kill you!"

I tackled him on top of the bed, throwing punches at his face and ribs. He just laughed as he tried to block them, thinking it was just some kind of joke. To think I could have... With *Tom*, of all people. I just wanted to throw up or kill something. Probably both.

Even though I was beating him up, Tim still laughed. "Wow, you are feisty in the bedroom. Jack must be kinky."

I threw punch after punch. "Shut up! Where is he? Tell me right now!"

"Gone," a voice said from behind me. I turned to find Joss and Logan standing in the doorway. Why did they have to be here? Why couldn't I just kill Tim in peace?

There was always someone stopping me.

"Gone? What do you mean?" I asked.

"I killed him the moment we came to this time," Joss said. "You think I would let him live after he stole my girl away from me? After making you go against me? I would never let that happen again."

The words hit me like a wall. It couldn't be true. It just couldn't't. Jack couldn't be dead, there was no way I was that unlucky. There was no way he could be killed that easily.

But then, where was he? Why wasn't he here? And why would Joss lie about something like that?

I shook my head. "You are lying!"

"No, Myra, I'm not. And now you have proven to me you can't be trusted. Logan, Tim, lock her up. I will come deal with her later."

I kept shaking my head. Logan and Tim started for me. "No," I shut my eyes. "Just stop!"

What happened next I never figured out. When I opened my eyes, I found everything frozen. Not in the ice-sort of sense, but like in time. They just stood there like statues, not moving, almost like mannequins. I blinked a couple of times, but they still didn't move. I didn't know what to do, or how it happened, but I knew this was my only chance to get out of there. I turned and headed to the door.

As I left, I found Dan coming towards the room. He

saw the frozen men standing there and gasped. "What happened? What did you do?"

I shook my head, crying now because of Jack and not knowing what exactly was going on. "They killed Jack. They killed him."

He looked even more surprised by this than the frozen men. "What? But Tim..."

"Isn't Jack. They tricked me. I made them stop, and now." I burst into tears. I never showed sadness around anyone, but I couldn't stop now. Jack was the only thing I cared for, and he was gone.

Dan wrapped his arms around me. "It's okay, sweetie. Just listen to me, okay? Run. Get away from here. I don't know how long whatever you did to them will last. You have to go." He mumbled a few words into my ears that a second later I didn't remember what those words were.

I nodded, and I ran down the corridor as fast as I could and found a ship.

Then I left Anosira.

Chapter 18

I ditched the ship I left Anosira with as fast as I could. Joss and the others would have been able to find me with it, though they'd have a bit of a tougher time since the Empire's control wasn't so large yet. If this was the future, if I had ever tried running away like this, I would have had no place to go. Well, other than Valle, but the moment I got near there I would have been shot out of the sky, so I guess I didn't have anywhere to go at this point.

So I landed on the closest planet, which was Cisum, and bought a Class One, a public transportation ship, ticket to Recar.

Why I wanted to torture myself even more about Jack, I had no idea. Everything on Recar would remind me of him and I would keep hearing his voice as other

Recarians were chatting all around me. Their accents were always so thick that many people sounded the same unless you really listened. I never thought I would miss that voice, miss always trying my hardest not to pick up the way they talked, but now I desired it more than ever.

I couldn't believe that he was dead, after all this time. I wanted to curl up and cry, but no more tears would leave my body. I felt dead inside, as if it was a struggle to keep on going. I had lost the only person who cared about me, who knew me and still cared about me regardless of my past offenses. And it hurt worse than any torture that has ever been bestowed on me.

I had always told myself not to grow attached to anyone since it would cause more pain and more complications during missions. I had believed I was successful and that Jack and I had a relationship where we didn't worry about the other, that if something happened, it was just part of life. That was what I had told my brother, and why he needed to let go of his worry for Amanda. He needed to realize more important things were at stake. Now I realized I was in the same boat, that every logical decision had left my mind. I didn't know if things changed when we were on Sanshli, that I started caring for him more, or if I had been lying to myself this entire time. Either way, I was in a lot of pain and didn't know if it would ever subside.

Even with this pain, I still didn't understand my brother's rash decisions, how he could do the things he was doing. Yes, restoring balance to the universe and destroying Nygard could bring back Amanda, but that didn't mean killing innocent people in the past would solve anything. Although I wanted to punch someone, mainly Tim and Joss, and was glad I got a few punches in with Tim before they stopped me. Nevertheless, I wouldn't start a full-blown war like my brother was doing right now.

I wondered if all this was done, if Jack would be okay. How did that even work, anyway? I didn't want to get my hopes up though; I was never one to hope for things, especially after watching Father be murdered right in front of me. I didn't hope that I would see him again, because there was a high chance that my hope would be crushed. I couldn't stand hearing he was dead twice in my life. So I wouldn't have hope, I would just do the things that could bring them back, but realize that it will not go the way I wanted it to.

The ship started its way to Recar, and I checked out the ship. It had been a while since I was on a Class One ship. I also needed some clothes, as the ones I was wearing were the only ones that I had with me, and with Recar being a six-day trip away, I needed something else to wear. It felt weird, looking for something to wear on a ship, as I never picked out my clothes before. Everything was given to me by one person or another. Jack had bought me clothes once, but I told him never to do it again. I didn't want to be caught dead wearing what he had bought me. Then again, he said it was just for him to see.

I shouldn't have thought about Jack. I was trying to

get through this, to get away from everything. Now I was just sad again. I didn't know what to do; I didn't know what I should do next. I was heading to Recar, and from there I was clueless. I still had the gem with me as it was in my pocket with my watch before I ran away. I still had to defeat Nygard, restore peace, and so on, and so on. Dan had taught me enough that I could train on my own, I knew. Well, at least for the elements—there were a lot of other things I could do with my powers that I didn't know.

Then there was what happened right before I ran away, when everyone froze for a millisecond. I didn't know how that happened—how I could make time appear to stop, yet other than those in the room, time just kept going on. Had it been me that did that? Was I able to do such things, being an Illusionist? I couldn't think that I was capable of such things; that I had been so angry, so distraught, that I could even stop time itself.

So had I been wrong this entire time? Should I have been using my emotions as my strength instead of seeing it as a weakness?

There were so many things going through my mind, things that I didn't want to think about. Yet I was doomed to ponder on them, let them observe me in what I was doing. The realization that I was capable of such power made me wish I didn't run away, that I stayed with Dan so he could train me in such things. But he was the one who pushed me to talk to Tim, whom I thought was my love, only to find out I had been tricked, that it was all a set up.

So did Dan know? He didn't seem to when he ran to the room after I had frozen everything. He was as surprised as me, and he let me run and get away from all that was happening, to gather myself up once again and keep fighting.

If that was even possible.

I ended up just buying some plain t-shirts and adequate pants for fighting, and some underwear. I also got a bag that I could store things in. I was able to steal some credits off of some gentlemen who were easily distracted by the events happening outside the port. It didn't surprise me that such people didn't keep a close watch on their money, as they had much to spare. So I would be good for quite some time now.

As I stepped outside the store, I took a deep breath. Joss would kill me if he ever found me. I was good at hiding and he knew that it all just depended on if he could read my mind. Which he couldn't anymore. So I should be good, if just for a while, anyway. That was all that mattered, to get some breathing room, to take in what had happened. Then I could finish what I had started—finish finding Sanshli.

I headed towards the dining hall. I didn't feel like eating, but I didn't feel like standing around feeling sorry for myself. Later I would find somewhere to exercise, like a gym. If I was lucky, maybe they would have a boxing arena where I could take out a few people. Maybe that would help with the stress.

The dining hall was busy, which I figured it would be at this time of day. Some people made it the goal to stay in here every hour they were awake to get all the deals they could for food. I was never big on food, as long as I had a meal I was fine. That could do with the time I spent at the Kamps, having times where I would be starved for days.

I still did not know why I had that stupid mark on my wrist. I was in a different body, and yet it was still there. Then again, it could have to do with me morphing into another person, that was still me, instead of being thrown into a new body as the others had. Either way, it wasn't fair. I wanted the mark to be gone; I didn't want to remember the horror I had witnessed there. I swore fate was playing some cruel trick with me. For all I knew, the mark could have been all in my head, just my paranoia.

No, Dan had seen it too. He had asked me what it was for.

Grabbing a seat at the bar, I grabbed a menu and ordered a smoky whiskey. I knew a beer wasn't hard enough and needed something to dull the pain. As for what I would do later, knowing I couldn't mask the pain forever, I wasn't sure. Probably running, running far, far away from anything familiar and focusing on completing my mission without the support of anyone.

The bartender gave me my drink, after carding me, for which I was glad my age was older on it than I was. It came in handy for some things like this. I then ordered some hummus as it was the only thing that sounded good at the moment. If I did have a preference, it was definitely healthier food. Junk food just always gave me a stomach ache.

A couple moments later, a plate of food appeared in front of me. I thanked him and dipped some veggies in the hummus. Taking a bite, I sighed. It tasted... plain. Hummus gave one so many possibilities, yet most of the time it was always plain, especially in restaurants like this.

Though I didn't know if it was because it was a horrible restaurant or if it was because of how I felt. Everyone around me seemed to enjoy it, maybe it was just me, or maybe they had a bit too much to drink already. Whatever it was, I didn't care. I just couldn't wait to get off this ship.

As I picked at my food, one man sat down next to me and also ordered some whiskey. I guess it was the best thing they had, which wouldn't surprise me if this ship was owned by Recar authorities. The Recarians were the best at making whiskey, and any other type of hard alcohol.

"So," the man turned to me. "Where do you come from?"

I glanced over at him. He reminded me a lot of Jack, the way he grinned, his messy black hair, his scruffy face. His clothes were well worn as well. If I didn't know Jack was dead, I would have thought for a moment he was Jack sent to the past. But Joss said he killed him, so that wasn't possible.

I took a sip of my drink. I didn't want to deal with anyone like him, or anyone at all. "None of your business, now is it?"

He laughed. They always laughed when I made such blunt statements. It was strange, as if they thought it was some kind of challenge.

"Ouch, I was just trying to start up a conversation with you."

I shook my head. "Not interested."

"How do you know before you even talk to me? Before you even know my name?"

Turning to him, I frowned. Creeps like him were all the same, pushing until they thought I would crack. Usually by now I would have walked away but we were on a ship, I couldn't leave unless I jumped out the airlock which wasn't sounding half bad at the moment.

"Look," I began. "I'm not interested in you, in anyone here, nor anyone in the future. I just want to be left alone, all right? So leave, before I punch that cocky grin off your pathetic face."

He rubbed the scruff on his face. "Well, well. Someone must have broken your heart."

Now he was going to analyze me? Fine, I would play his game and make him feel bad about it. "I just found out he was murdered. So *back off*."

His eyes widened, as if he didn't think that would be my answer. Few people would bluntly say that their love had been killed. I would though, but then again I was used to being surrounded by death, though this one stung more than I could have ever imagined.

"Oh... I didn't realize. Here, let me buy you a drink."

I couldn't believe he was still trying. Whoever he was, he must have dealt with this situation before. If I wasn't so preoccupied, I might have tried to figure out what that was. But I knew at the moment it would be a waste of time.

"I already have a drink," I said. "What I want is to be alone. Understand? Alone."

He picked up his whiskey and left me alone. *Thank goodness.* I didn't want to punch him in the nose. Well... I did, but I didn't want to get in trouble for it and have to worry about my brother seeing me on the news. Or Joss. Or anyone, if I was honest. That would be my luck, being caught because I couldn't control my anger. I was surprised that didn't happen.

I wondered if my brother was searching through video cams for me with facial recognition programs. It would be hard since the galaxy was so large, and the fact Recar didn't like the Republic spying on them. Or anyone. In fact, if I recalled my history well enough, the first time security cameras were put on Recar, different gang members used them as target practice.

Luckily, the footage from the cameras rarely lasted a week.

Though, as of now, they were still sided with the Republic, but that would change soon. I wondered if they would still become independent when the time came, though at this point in time they were independent. The Republic just kind of let it slide as long as the time came, that they would bear arms to help the Republic when need be.

Problem was that they didn't, but started a rebellion to free themselves from the entire messy system. Sounded about right, knowing them. I guess you could say they were autonomous.

But that was up in the air. This timeline had changed, between Wes being an idiot and Joss focusing on finding Sanshli and bringing destruction upon the Republic, probably wanting to squash it under his foot more so than the actual Emperor from this time did. He wouldn't let anyone start up the P.A.E., wouldn't let any Republic sympathizers escape his wrath.

And who could blame him? It was why we were here, because some stupid idiot pulled out the sword and sent us in the past to battle it out once again. And just to be clear, that stupid idiot was my brother.

I finished up my hummus, or at least how much I wanted to eat of it, and went to the room I had purchased to stay in. It was more decorated, very artificially might I add, than any room I had ever had since I was taken from Garvner as a child. I wanted to rip it all away, but I also didn't have that much money to cover the charges I would receive if I did such a thing.

Sighing, I fell onto the bed. I wanted to sleep forever, but knew that sleep would never come to me, not to mention I would just be plagued with a series of dreaded nightmares. I glanced up at the mirror in my room. It was strange, I hadn't seen Violet since I had left Anosira, after we had that argument about my powers and Nygard. I didn't know if she was mad at me or if something happened—if anything really could happen. She was a ghost projected through time. How could she disappear? I guess it was possible that she had lost the remnants of her power just as Brayen did. I prayed that wasn't the case, as I knew I still needed her help, needed to figure out how to use the gem to find Sanshli. She wouldn't just leave me now like this, would she? I doubted it. It was probably just because we had argued. She wanted to let me cool off.

I pulled out my pocket watch and stared at it, letting my mind resonate with the ticking noise, but it seemed impossible. There was too much going on in my head. I wanted it all to stop, wanted it all to go away. But it wasn't going to, it wouldn't end, ever. I needed to stand tall, I needed to finish this for once and for all.

And that's what I would do after training on Recar.

Chapter 19

The ship landed at the port outside the city of Himeo. The city looked the same as it did in the future, the same buildings, chaotic streets, underground rail system that made very little sense to the normal person. At least it could get you where you needed to go, as long as you knew it well enough because quite frankly it was like a maze. To the tourist, however, it was practically impossible. I loved watching people pull out maps and try to figure it out, curse a bunch out loud as they had missed their exit and would have to either reroute or get off and go back. Very entertaining to say the least.

I wondered if the reason the transportation was so screwed up had to do with Recar being independent, wanting to maintain their way of life, so they don't bother to change anything or make sure it was orderly. I knew Jack wouldn't bother adding buildings or changing streets unless he had to, which meant it had to have been blown up or something. There just was too much paperwork involved.

Ah, that's what it was. Paperwork. Ironic for a 'business man' to hate paperwork.

So they would rebuild buildings if they got damaged in some kind of brawl, but they would make them almost the same as they were before. Which made me wonder how many times each building had been damaged and then restored.

I made my way on the underground train and listened as stop after stop was being called by the automatic speaker. I knew all the names by heart, knew where each one led, where the different connections were. I didn't have anywhere I wanted to go, nowhere in particular, but once the name 'Dragon' was called, I stepped off and head up to the street. Why that name stood out from the others, I wasn't sure. It could have been just because the fact a stop was named 'Dragon' stood out to me, as it reminded me of Sanshli with the statues of dragons guarding the building that Nygard had been placed in. Maybe it was a sign that somewhere near this exit may just help me figure out how to find Sanshli after all.

Yeah, if I could ever be that lucky.

I wondered if I could find a place to stay around here, until I made my way into the hills just outside town, past where all the bandits lived, because I knew that they were out there, waiting for some unsuspecting traveler to rob. Maybe for the heck of it I would rob them, give them a little taste of their own medicine. Though it was something I would do, I didn't feel up to it, not with everything going on.

I needed supplies though, I wouldn't go out there empty handed. There was nothing out there, no shops or restaurants that I could visit if I needed to. I would have to be prepared.

One problem was to do that, I would need money. Sure, I had pick-pocketed a man earlier to get on the ship, but this was Recar we were talking about. There weren't as many people that were easily tricked as there were in the rest of the galaxy. These people were used to pick-pockets, common thieves, gangs, so forth. I would have to be very careful if I wanted to find money. I would need to find a tourist that didn't have a bunch of locks on their credits. Most knew of the seedy reputation of Recar, they knew the risk if they didn't make sure their credits were secure on them.

The best place I could find money was at a bar. At least the men there were drunk and were easily distracted by a woman. I would keep an eye out for a bar that looked good to try my thieving skills at as I walked around. I would have to go to a few bars to get enough money though. Staying at one would just be a death sentence if anyone figured it out.

At least I didn't have to worry about being considered a criminal here. It would just be part of daily life here.

I wandered the familiar streets, not paying attention to where I was going. I felt as if it was where I needed to go, a place my mind subconsciously took me. It was weird. It was a feeling I had since I left Anosira. A feeling in the back of my mind, as if it was taking me where I needed to go. I kept my head down while walking. I didn't feel like holding it up high, I felt like disappearing with the crowd.

Keeping on the blind path I was going, I felt my body stop. I wasn't sure why, it just felt like my legs didn't want to keep moving, like I needed to be where I was. I looked up to find I had stopped in front of a small pub. It was quaint, with the name 'Royal Straight' in red neon lights plastered on the side. It looked like an enjoyable place to play cards, but sometimes looks were deceiving. It could just be a plain bar that wanted to have a gambling feel without the paperwork needed to run such a thing.

That is, if they ran it legally. There were probably a few rooms in the back. There always were.

It was underground, at least the entrance was down some stairs. It made it even more conspicuous, as if only a few brave souls that weren't criminals would ever enter this bar.

Which felt like the perfect place to hang out and pickpocket some people.

I stepped down the stairs, still debating if this was a good idea or not. It was raining, thundering behind me, just like the last time I was on Recar. At least this time I didn't have a crime lord trying to kill me. Well, not yet anyways.

Taking a deep breath, I turned the door knob and stepped inside.

"Sorry, we aren't open yet. Come back later." A young waitress came from the back kitchen. Her hair was red with tight curls, and she had a thin face. Her cheeks were covered with freckles and I didn't think she could be a day over seventeen.

I should have noticed it was still morning. I was all messed up from the space ride here, not thinking about the time change. For me it was almost dinner time. "Sorry, I don't know what brought me here. I should have noticed you weren't open, it's still morning."

I started for the door when I heard another person come out from the back.

"Wait!" the man called after me. I turned to find a tall, dark haired man standing in the doorway. He just stared at me, gaping. Why he was looking at me like that, I did not know. I just stood there, raising an eyebrow.

"Yeah? What is it?" I asked, not sure why some random guy would stop me from leaving a bar that wasn't even open yet. It seemed strange, which made me curious and was why I didn't just turn and walk away.

He stepped closer to me, silent. His eyes were a beautiful shade of blue, ones I could stare at for hours. Not many people had that color blue, and I always admired it. It seemed almost supernatural in a way.

The man smiled after a moment. "Cadi?"

My eyes widened. Only one person would ever call me that. Even though I thought it wasn't possible, it had to be him. It had to. "Jack!"

Chapter 20

I didn't hesitate as I ran and jumped into Jack's arms. He was taller, and it was odd being in love with a person in a different body, even though at least this time I knew it was him. He had recognized me, against all odds.

His arms wrapped around my body. He was still just as strong; I could feel it. His face was scruffy as usual and his hair as shaggy as ever. It didn't matter what century we were in, he would keep to the same look, but I knew he could pull anything off. He had that kind of distinct demeanor. The 'say anything about how I look that isn't good and I will kill you' demeanor that I always liked about him. It was also why he insisted his nickname was 'Handsome Jack', not 'Crazy Jack' like everyone called him when he wasn't around.

I started crying, tears soaking his already dirty dress

shirt. It made me feel weak, but at this moment I didn't care. My love was back from the dead. I had found him, against all odds. "They told me you were dead. They said they killed you."

He stroked my back. "Shhh, don't worry, I'm here. It's okay. They could never kill me."

The strangest part of the change was hearing a different voice. His Recarian accent was still there. But this voice was unfamiliar. This voice more direct, if that was the word. It was crisp and to the point. It was still Jack's, though, and that was all that mattered to me.

I let him hold me in his arms. His shirt dried up the tears I shed. Tears for the past year I was away from him. The past year where I didn't know if he was alive or dead. It all came out, every tear I repressed. Every tear I denied. I never cried, I never had reason to. Not until I heard Joss say those words I had always feared. That he had killed him. It was a lie, but I didn't know that then. If he could, Joss would have killed Jack years ago. If he foresaw this, he wouldn't have even hesitated.

I was glad he said nothing about how I was in this state, a state I never thought I would find myself in. After Father died in front of my eyes, after enduring what I did in the Kamps, I didn't think I could shed another tear of sadness. I thought I had endured all that I could, that there was no way my body could endure it any longer, as if my emotions had turned off. I guess that was a lie I just told myself, a lie that I thought I was protecting myself with.

Jack looked up at the barmaid. I thought about

commenting on how she looked like the secretaries he used to have, but decided not to. I didn't want to start that fight up again, though when I thought this I swore I heard him chuckle a little.

"Jane," Jack began. "You and the rest have the day off, go let the others know. I'm not opening today. I'll pay you all your salary. Just let us be alone all right?"

She gave me a suspicious look, as if she couldn't understand why I was so important. I trusted Jack did nothing with her, he knew I could kill him in so many ways, though that didn't mean she didn't want his attention.

"All right, see you later Mister Vanguard." She turned and entered the kitchen. Jack kept me close as the workers left, stroking my hair.

"I missed you so much," he whispered into my ear after everyone left. We could talk about what had happened without worrying about anyone overhearing and wondering what we were. I know if I heard two people chatting about time travel, and that someone was from the future, I would try to listen in.

Jack went on. "I thought about looking for you but I didn't know where to start. Figured if I stayed put, you would find me. Guess I was right."

I took a deep breath to gather myself. I let my weakness show and now it was time to put it all back away. Go back to the person I was, someone who was strong enough to fight anything. "I wasn't looking for you, I thought you were dead. For some reason, my intuition led me here. Pure happenstance."

Jack pulled me back and looked at me, as if he was trying to figure something out. How I could have found him, I had no idea. I wondered if he thought I was lying, that I had known this whole time or something. After a moment, he smiled. "Let us catch up." He pulled me to a booth and sat me down. "Tell me what happened."

I closed my eyes. So much had happened since I last saw him, between being with my brother and with Joss. Yet it felt just like yesterday when I woke up in this time. "A lot. Jack, I don't even know where to begin." But I gave it a shot, anyway. "We were transported back in time."

"I gathered that. New body and everything."

I laughed. I missed how sarcastic and cocky he was. We were like two peas in a pod. "Now you know how I felt on Sanshli. When I first woke up, Rik was Wes."

Jack rubbed his chin. "The leader of the Republic? *Chancellor* Wesley Atkins?"

I nodded. "Then Will and David are his generals. I was a 'general', if that is what you could call it. It felt more like I was a prisoner of war, but what could I expect? My brother hasn't ever trusted me, not after he found out I was the Empire's Shadow. I was there for a while but Rik was pissing me off so I left and find the Empire. I knew Neil would be waiting for a chance to get me alone, to get me to come back so he could use my powers. I let that happen. I was there for a little while. I thought..." I paused, not wanting him to know what happened with Tom. "I thought you were with them. I found out you weren't, and Neil said he killed you. Then I ran."

He bit his lip, watching as I thought about what Tom had done, lying about being Jack. I didn't want to tell him what had happened, ashamed that I could have been fooled so easily. That, and the fact I almost slept with Tom.

"They lied to you just like that? Just to see if you would give up everything for me?" he asked.

I blinked. I had never said he was the reason I ran away, that I had risked being punished to tell him I loved him, or Tim who was pretending to be Jack. I had thought it, yes, but I knew for a fact that I had said nothing out loud. "What?"

Realization of what he had said was apparent on his face. He knew he spoke too soon, that he let it slip out.

Which meant only one thing.

"Cadi—"

I frowned. "You can read minds, can't you?"

He nodded. Of all the powers, it had to be that one, the one I dread the most, the one that was the most painful to deal with. Yes, I could try to mask my thoughts—try to hide them from everyone around, because at this point I doubted there was a person out there who couldn't read my mind. But it grew tiresome, just another thing to worry about, to have to be conscious about.

Why couldn't people just stick to their own minds? Why did it always have to be that they were reading the minds of others, especially when they have the coveted ability?

"That's all I need, another person in my mind." I rubbed my forehead. Why everything kept getting more and more complicated, I had no idea. I just wanted it all to simmer down and settle, but it didn't seem like that would ever happen. "So then you know what happened with Tim."

Jack rubbed the back of his neck, as if thinking of the best way to deal with him. If I knew Jack, which I did, I could guess all the fun things he would do with him, which he would let me take part in. "I'm going to kill him the next time I see him."

Though I agreed, it wasn't his idea. It was Joss'. "It wasn't just him, he was ordered to act like you."

"Yeah, I'm sure he protested."

I didn't blame him for wanting to kill Tim, I was right there with him. But there was a lot more at stake. We had to defeat Nygard, we have so much to do before we could think about petty revenge. But if the time came, I would want revenge. "What are we going to do next, Jack?"

He bit his lip and closed his eyes for a moment. As he opened them, he pointed at my pocket. "Let me see that gem."

Instead of asking me about everything, he just read my mind. Everyone seemed to enjoy doing that as of late— act as if talking to me was too much trouble. Jack was just having fun with it, finally able to see what's going on inside my mind. I know he had always been curious, as I was never opened to anyone. This was a dream come true for him.

I sighed as I handed him the gem. "It can tell us where Sanshli is, problem is I don't know how to use it. All I know is that the darkest light will show the location. So maybe if we shine a light through it? But what the darkest light is, I do not understand."

He inspected it, as if I hadn't already done so to look for clues. There was nothing on it, nothing in it. It looked like an ordinary gem to me. Maybe Violet was mistaken. Maybe this gem was a decoy, and the other had been stolen. Seemed unlikely though, as it was enclosed in the hollow brick.

After Jack found nothing strange about the gem, he handed it back to me. "We will figure it out, don't worry Cadi."

I missed being called Cadi, that name that had been taken away from me a year ago. No one called me Arcadia, other than Wes, which had more to do with his stubbornness than it did caring that my life was a lie, that I wasn't the person I once thought I was. Jack made that all go away, though. He made me feel like I was myself once again.

"Worry?" I asked. "I have to defeat Nygard, Jack. You think that will be easy? You think I can defeat a legend?"

He grabbed my hand and kissed my fingers, his lips gentle even though I knew he didn't want them to be. It took him a lot of restraint, as it always did. "I think you can do anything, if you set your mind to it."

I rolled my eyes.

"Well, I will always be at your side. You can count on that. Your wish is my command." He did a brief bow, as if he was some kind of gentleman or something. Though, out of everyone I knew, he was a gentleman in public. He knew all the things he needed to do to get a woman to like him. It was... concerning, though I liked it sometimes. Lance came in at a close second though, as he was just polite to anyone. In his case, it made him weak and an easy target for some while for Jack it made him even more cunning. I would never outright admit that to him and I hid that thought in my mind before he could read it.

I sighed. "What we need to do is hide this. If I know Neil, which I do, then he will come looking for me. He will find out about the gem, especially if Dan reveals I had disappeared for a few minutes on Ttkas to get it. And then, after we are ready and find Sanshli, we must get everyone to go there together, then defeat Nygard and those that serve him."

"Oh, is that all? Sounds simple," Jack teased.

"Yeah, as easy as it has been for the past year. So easy," I commented. I couldn't wait until it was all over. This mission felt like it was going on forever. Though, in hindsight, it had been going on for thousands of years. This was just our end of it, I couldn't imagine all that Brayen and Violet had gone through for this, to keep the universe at peace.

Jack added. "Getting your brother to do anything will be an interesting experience."

Ugh. I didn't even want to think about my brother and trying to get him to do anything for me. He didn't think with a straight mind. I swore his brain was just wired for idiocy now. "Don't even get me started. But I can tell him it's the only way to end this, the only way to get Amanda back. Then he will go."

"Wouldn't you if it were to save me?"

I didn't know how to answer that. Yes, when I thought he was dead, I hoped that maybe if I found Sanshli, if I could go back to the future, that he would be alive and well. But I didn't want to get my hopes up, I didn't want to become obsessed with one thing only to find out that wasn't the truth, that I lost him and that there was no way to get him back. I had worked so hard to let my emotions be drowned out by logic that I wasn't one to go on such idealistic quests like my brother was doing.

I fidgeted with my fingers. "You know I would go after Sanshli either way. But I wouldn't get my hopes up. I know that life sometimes doesn't go how we plan. But as for the gem, I have no idea where we should hide it to be sure it's safe."

We sat there silently thinking. Then Jack started laughing.

"What is it?" I asked, wondering what idiotic place he could have thought of. This was how our missions went, with him concocting some plan, even though it would be a death trap, and then I would go along with it, anyway. It always ended up okay, for the most part.

"How well can you control your powers?" he asked.

I shrugged. Honestly, I didn't think I was that great, as Dan had only two days to train me. I needed more training for sure, but I was capable of something now. "All right. I'm figuring it out. Why?"

He grinned. "Then I know the perfect place to put it. The safest place in all the systems, at least for a while.

Just trust me."

I hated it when he made that smile and told me to trust him. It meant that we would get in a lot of trouble if they caught us.

Yet I could never say no.

Chapter 21

Of course, *that* was what Jack thought up. He was such an idiot. I swore I was surrounded by idiots. But then again, I had come up with some ridiculous plans in the past. But this one outdid them tenfold.

Jack wanted me to figure out if I could use my powers to place the gem inside something solid. And what was that solid thing? Oh, right, it was the trophy for the Recar Races.

Yes, the races even existed way back when. They had to have existed since Recar became habitable. Crime lords and races, that's what this planet was all about.

I didn't know if that made this planet more fun or if it made it more ridiculous. I just couldn't be sure. Probably both, as Jack was giddy with excitement to be involved in the races once more. Quirky didn't even describe him,

I swore.

So I concentrated on making solids morph into each other, without ruining the gem. I had a feeling if the gem was something from Sanshli, then there was no way that it would be destroyed so easily. Which was a good thing, though I still would be careful. I didn't want my only chance of going home to be ruined because I messed up. That is, if I had a home, and if we would get sent back into the future. It was all up for debate, but I knew the only way to find out was by finishing this mission once and for all.

I sat at the bar, trying to put peanuts through a beer bottle. Yes, seriously. Jack figured it would be the same as putting a gem in a trophy base. I didn't quite see his logic in that, but I never understood his logic. Ever.

Not to mention so far I hadn't gotten it to work. It was frustrating. I just wished Dan was around, helping me. He would have put a gun to my head and told me to do it before he pulled the trigger. I wondered if he would shoot me a second time though.

"Who's Dan?" Jack asked as he cleaned up some glasses that was in the sink. It was weird seeing him do such work, as he was a crime lord for this planet and always had someone else to do the dirty work while he, well, did dirty work.

I frowned and glared at him. "I told you to stop reading my mind."

"I was just curious about what you were thinking while you used your powers. I'm sorry, it won't happen again, I promise."

For some reason, I didn't believe him.

"Yeah, whatever." I stared at the bottle and sighed. "Dan was just a trainer, he is better than anyone I have ever met at fighting."

"Even me?"

"You use unfair tactics most of the time. Dan doesn't use any weapons or any sort of cheap tricks. He just used sheer strength and smarts. He also taught me how to use my powers, if only for a couple of days. I wish I had learn more from him." And I meant that. Although his tactics were strange, I learned from him and I knew that if he was here, he could help me get the damn peanut inside the beer bottle.

"And shot you to do that? That doesn't seem like something an instructor should do. Not a credible one anyways."

"Seriously? Stop reading my mind."

"Last time."

"But yes, he shot me. And it worked. The next time we were out on that island, I could control different elements. But I'm still lacking. Logan made the surrounding fire disappear. I have so much to learn." And it was true, I had so much to learn and now I had no one to teach me. I had no one to help me.

"I could teach you, and instead of punishing you if you fail, I could most definitely reward you," Jack gave me one of his famous winks.

I rolled my eyes. "Really? Gonna make jokes like that?"

He just laughed. "Sorry, Cadi, I forgot you liked it

rough. You like to be punished rather than get a reward."

Sad to say, he probably was right. I got myself in a lot of messes over the years, but I never looked for a reward after it all. I just wanted to show that I was tough enough to defeat anything, and if I failed, then I would most definitely have died, if not just get seriously injured.

And that always excited me. Or maybe I just had a death wish. One couldn't be too certain.

"You think you could teach me?"

He stopped cleaning the mug he had in his hand and leaned against the table. "Yes, it's easy. I just have to tell you one thing."

"Oh? And what's that?"

"If you fail, Nygard will destroy you. And me. He could come walking through that door at any second, and you need to beat him now. Not later. Now. If you don't do this, we are all screwed. We will all die. Stop thinking about all the others that have been in the way and think of your goal—of whom you have to defeat. You don't know when, you don't know how powerful he is, so you need to get your act together and focus on being as strong as you can be to save your own ass. Got it?"

I stared at him. He was right, I didn't think of this as being in the present, I just kept thinking about how I would defeat Nygard in the future. I needed to think about the present, that this second could be our last. That if I didn't become as powerful as I could at once, I could lose it all.

But could Nygard walk through that door at any

second? Where had he been this entire time? It seemed strange to me we hadn't run into him if he was free of his prison on Sanshli, that there was no word of him being alive anywhere. Where would he go first? If I was him, what would I do first?

I would look for my daughter who was supposed to bring my destruction. Yeah, that was what I would do. So I needed to get my act together fast.

I grabbed the peanut, and I didn't think about anything. I just knew that it could go through the glass because I wanted it to. I was a Sanshlian, I was the daughter of the most powerful Illusionist throughout time itself. Anything was possible.

And it worked. The peanut went through the glass and fell to the bottom of the empty bottle.

Smiling, I looked over at Jack. It was the petty things that made me want to boast, though I hadn't decided whether this feat was little or big. It was complicated, I gave it that.

"Good job," Jack said. "Now get it out."

I sighed. Here I thought I had accomplished so much only to have to start all over again.

After cutting my fingers on the glass, because apparently one couldn't lose their focus as they put their hand through glass or they are in for a lovely treat, I got the peanut out. Jack got me some bandages, though it wasn't long before they were healed. I held the bloody peanut up in triumph.

"Ah ha! I did it!"

"You should probably practice it a few more times before we break into the most highly secured building of Recar."

"Don't you find it sad that the highest security building on Recar is where they keep the trophy for the races?" Because I sure did. I mean, who in their right mind thought 'oh, here's a trophy for some races, we should build a fortress for it to make sure no one will steal it'. Then again, it was Recar and there were many, many thieves lurking around. I couldn't blame the developers of such a fortress in the slightest.

"Oh, Cadi, it makes perfect sense. The trophy is one of the most expensive things on this planet. Whoever wins it melts it down and can feed and clothe their family for life, not to mention they can get a job with someone like me."

Memories of the first time we met came flooding back to me. In order to get close to Jack, I had entered the races. "That's right, that's how I ended up with you in the first place. But we know it wasn't just my skill that you were interested in."

Jack smiled. "It's not every day some girl comes and beats all the big shots in town, not to mention no one had ever heard of her."

"Which brings us to the trophy. How are we going to get it back?" I asked.

"Easy, you will win the races. Or I will since I am Xander Vanguard, the racer who was said to have murdered the current leader and take over Recar during this time period."

I couldn't believe what I was hearing. First off, how did he remember that history lesson when a lot of Recar's history was muddled. Second, did he really think we had enough time to wait for the races that wouldn't happen for a few months from now? I guess it gave us time to train, for me to learn more about my powers. Maybe by then, I will know just where Nygard was.

"You think that's a good idea?" I asked. Although I had won it in the past, I didn't know what the competition would be like here, whether I could win. Although I trusted that we could beat whoever it was we were up against, I didn't want to worry about messing up.

"It will be fine, Cadi, there are two of us. If one of us messes up, then the other will win. Besides, if someone else wins, we will just follow them and take the gem out of the trophy. Easy as that."

I tapped my finger on the table. He had a point. There were other ways we could retrieve the gem. "Then we will have to hightail it to Sanshli. With everyone." I rubbed my forehead. I forgot the part where we needed to make sure everyone would be on Sanshli. It just kept getting more and more complicated. "How is that going to work?"

"What, do I have to come up with everything? Besides, we have time to figure that out. The races aren't for another four months. They haven't even closed the registration to enter. We still have a month to sign up."

I kind of wondered how he knew that, as if he was already thinking about entering. It wouldn't have surprised me that he was so bored that he wanted to join the races. "Good point, there's a lot going on that we don't understand. Hopefully we figure it out by then."

Jack nodded. "Agreed. So keep practicing, then we will do this for real."

"Yeah, I know. Practice a billion more times so I perfect it. Sound like Dan. I think his favorite word is 'again'."

He laughed as he turned on the television. Recarian news was definitely more entertaining than that of any other planet's news. Always about murder cases, rivals, and then sometimes about an old lady with lots of cats. Very diverse and interesting. I hated listening to the news anywhere else, but here it was like it kept your interest instead of informing you of what was happening. Let's be honest, no one here cared about each other's affairs unless they were good gossip.

As I tried to get the peanut to go through the glass again, something on the screen caught my eye. A dark-haired man was on the screen, one that I had seen before. "Wait. Who is that?"

Jack glanced up. "Oh, him? Don't you know your Recarian history? He is the head of Himeo and is securing the trophy as we speak. He is that one that is supposed to get assassinated by yours truly, if we follow history that is."

I let out a laugh. It was the man who hit on me on the Class One ship. It was the guy that reminded me of Jack, and now I knew why. "I think I know how we will get in the building."

Chapter 22

Jack hated my idea, though he hated most ideas that I came up with when they involved hitting on other men. But it was the best way to get in. Crime lords were easily manipulated, when you knew what to do, and I could handle myself against him or any of his lackeys. I was stronger than before, after Dan's training, not to mention I now had powers.

And Jack had my back, as he always did on Recar and pretty much anywhere. I was glad to have him on my side because if he wasn't, I would have one formidable opponent on my hands.

Jack, for some odd reason, had a dress that fit me perfectly. I asked him why he had such a dress and he swears that it was because he saw it and it reminded him of me so he bought it. It all sounded a little fishy, but I doubted Jack would ever lie to me. He just wasn't the type of guy who would cheat on someone they loved.

Usually.

I put my short, curve-hugging black dress on, did my hair in curls, which I hadn't done for a long while. Hair curlers sucked. I always burnt myself, but at least I could heal faster now. And I usually hid my fingers with gloves. Not this time though. He wouldn't know what the barcode was for, as the Kamps hadn't been created... yet. It would be a few more years. I thought about making sure Joss didn't make them again, but it really didn't matter at this point. All that mattered was finding Sanshli and stopping all the horrible things associated with it from ever happening. Too much manipulation of past events for one's own devices would emulate too many bad traits of my brother, anyway.

Jack took me to the bar he figured the head of Himeo would be at. It was where the Himeo boss always hung out at night. I asked if that meant his enemies knew where he was. He just shrugged it off and said it was like a safe zone for each city. Yeah, like that made sense. Crime lords with codes they lived by. Whatever, I wasn't one to question things on this planet. I would never get a straight answer.

So here I was, heading towards the bar. I couldn't believe I had been so lucky to run into the head of Himeo. I wondered why he was taking just a public ship like that. He had a reason, wanting to lie low. Or just get away for a while, which seemed about as likely. I would ask, then I would have at least one thing to talk about.

I got to the bar. There were about five security guards were at the door, checking people for weapons and judging them to see if they were okay to go in. I got to the front of the line and the guard acted as if he would pat me down.

"Really?" I asked. "You can't tell that I have no weapons with this dress?"

He shrugged and still patted me down and checked my purse. The purse appeared to have just normal things in it: blush, tape, comlink, and lipstick.

Of course, the tape was so I could get the fingerprints to get into the most secured building in Himeo.

I made it sound like it would be easy to get into the building that held the trophies. It wasn't, but I had someone who knew the layout like the back of his hand, not to mention I could listen to the building, know where people waited for us inside it. All we needed were a few things to get in, such as access codes. Jack had the number, but he didn't have the right fingerprint.

And that's where this bar came in.

All I needed was his glass, and I was golden. It would be easy to get since all I needed was to have a couple of drinks with him and then leave the bar with the fingerprint on the tape. That was it. Easy.

Except plans never went how they were supposed to when I was in charge.

All the same, it would get done and we would have the gem in the trophy by morning. Then we could train and get ready to defeat Nygard. And, of course, figure out how we would get everyone to be on Sanshli.

The guard nodded, and I walked in.

It was loud. Really loud. Jack never had the music blaring at this volume when he was in charge. And it was not my type of music, and I liked a lot of music. Whatever, I would get over it.

I spotted him right away. He was at the bar talking to a couple of guys, probably some men who had a lot of power, through money or some sort. I walked up to the bar close to him, but not too close as to seem obvious.

As I ordered a whiskey, I could feel his eyes on me. So he remembered me. That was good. I just hoped he wouldn't be mad still I blew him off.

Then again, if he was like Jack, he would be persistent.

Just as I thought that, I saw him dismiss himself with his colleagues and walk over to me right as the bartender handed me my drink.

"Let me guess, a whiskey?" he asked as he leaned against the bar next to me.

I took a sip and turned to him. "Maybe it is." I waved the glass around to exaggerate where we were. "Quite a place. Wouldn't have guessed this was all yours."

He laughed as he took in the sights. "Not just this place, but the entire city and everything in it."

He was cocky as a certain crime lord I knew. I just hoped Jack didn't read my mind when I thought that, not that it mattered. He knew I thought he was cocky. It was just how people like him acted, and who could blame them. Look at all the power they had. Everyone did all they could to please them. Which, at times like this, made it much easier for me to get what I wanted.

"Everything in it you say?"

Grinning, he held out his hand. "We never introduced ourselves. I'm Kane Hullihan. I'm the leader of this city."

"Myra Ryetirf. Don't have an occupation, or much of anything at the moment. Just kind of making my way around the galaxy."

"You mean pick-pocketing your way across the galaxy?" he asked.

I raised an eyebrow. I was surprised that he had seen me, I was careful after all. "You saw that? How long have you been following me?"

"Just saw you at the port, that's all. Thought to myself, that is a girl I want to get to know. So when I saw you at the bar, I just couldn't resist."

If I had known who he was, had known that Jack was safe, I would have gone along with the act a little more. It would have made things so much easier. "Yeah, sorry about that. I wasn't in the greatest mood. I'm better now, I've had a while to think things through, to realize the truth of what had happened."

He watched my eyes suspiciously. "Didn't you say your love was murdered right in front of your eyes?"

Right, I forgot that I had mentioned that. Me and my big mouth. "Yes, but the part I left out was what kind of man my love was. He was dark and had hurt many people. The people who killed him were trying to bring justice to their city. I was supposed to be next, but I got away."

Kane laughed. "So what you're saying is that I have a wanted criminal in my city."

"Doesn't that describe all your citizens?"

"Citizens?" He let the word linger on his lips. "Thinking about staying here then?"

I shrugged. "I might, if given the right incentive. Heard you all have a race coming up. Sounds like fun." I took a sip of the whiskey. "And besides, the drinks you all have here are like no other. I might just stay for them."

"I hope that isn't your only reason," he smiled as he leaned closer.

"We will have to see, now won't we. But those races look like fun. Not every day you get to go so fast. I bet the adrenaline rush is to die for." I picked my words carefully, to make sure I had his attention, and I did. I could tell by the way he was looking at my lips, then letting his gaze slip down to my dress.

"You think you will enter?" he asked as he motioned to the bartender to bring him a drink. The bartender brought a glass of whiskey, neat. It was perfect.

"I just might. Just want to know what's in it for me." I moved my foot over to touch his leg.

He coughed. I must have caught him off guard, which was a little surprising. "Umm, well there is always the trophy which has a chief gold value. But then, if you win, I will see to it that you will work close to me."

"That sounds exciting, working close to you. I guess I will sign up then. Four months from now?" I asked as I took another sip.

Kane nodded. "Yeah."

"Well, I better start training then. Don't want to

disappoint you." I winked. Damn, I was too good at this. Logan was right about me. I would do anything for a mission to succeed. Well, almost anything.

He took a large gulp, finishing his drink.

I nodded over to his group. "As for now, you should get back to talking to your friends. You don't want to keep them waiting."

Kane stared at me for a moment longer, biting his lip. "You are right, I should. But we will see each other again, I will make sure of that, Myra. Until then."

He stepped away and went back to where the group of men were waiting for him. And, luckily, he left his empty glass at the bar. Jack was quick to come and pick it up, with gloved hands of course.

"You did that all too well, Cadi. Makes me worry," Jack whispered.

I laughed. "Don't worry, I usually only use those moves on you."

"I don't like how you used the word 'usually'."

I pulled out my blush and the tape I had in my purse. "Now, now, Jack. It's no time to get jealous. Just think of this as a means to an end."

"You better not just look at me as a means to an end."

Putting some blush on the glass where I saw a good fingerprint, I put some tape on it and pulled it off. Perfect fingerprint. "You know you are more than that. At least you are now."

"Right, I forgot. You tried to kill me when first met."

I gave him a little pout. "But I didn't, so all's good."

"You didn't kill me because I was one step ahead of

you," he commented, which was true. Jack had given me a run for my money and if he wasn't so interested in me, I would have been dead.

"That was a long time ago, you need to move on and be lucky that Neil never ordered me to kill you again. Now, let's get out of here before Kane comes back."

Chapter 23

We got back to Jack's bar with good timing. I wanted to change before we went to the building where the trophy was. Jack had all the codes memorized. Apparently, there was a pattern only those who ruled Himeo knew and he could backtrack to the present. They did odd things here.

I changed into a black tank top, black pants, and a black jacket with boots. Jack did the same. We had to be stealthy, in and out with no one noticing. Jack, at least, could read minds so he could listen for anyone who was coming and fight them knowing what they would do. I could use my powers a bit and would stop anyone we ran into.

Once we were ready, Jack, and I hurried out the door. This needed to happen tonight. We didn't know when Joss would come looking for me or when he would figure out where I went. I had a feeling coming here was his first thought. I had been stupid thinking he wouldn't look here. I still wasn't sure what drove me here, as there were plenty of other planets I could have gone to and never be found, such as Ttkas, though I would never be caught dead hiding on that planet. Nevertheless, I found Jack, and that was all that mattered for now.

The building was just as I remembered it, standing right in the middle of where the races always were held. The thought of attending the races excited me a little, as it had been such a long time. I wondered if I still could win. Probably, but there was just a little doubt in my mind.

I placed the thumbprint we had taken onto the keypad while Jack entered the code.

And it worked. We had been successful in getting in, now we just needed to be successful in getting to the trophies and getting out.

Which is where my powers and Jacks' powers would come in handy.

I could sense where people were in the building by listening to sounds coming through the walls and see what they were seeing. I had grown better at fine-tuning this ability. Now, I could focus on when Jack was in different parts of the bar and be able to pinpoint his location. Never had I dreamed I could do such a thing. If I had honed this power earlier in my life, many missions would have been a lot easier.

Maybe that was how my intuition had left me alive for all these years. Maybe I could have in fact sensed them, just not to this extent.

As we entered, I closed my eyes and focused. Jack knew where we needed to go, but I needed to make sure that there was no one waiting for us, no one to stop us as we were about to have our hand on one of the most valuable things on the planet.

It made me laugh every single time.

There were five guards between where we were and where we needed to go. We needed to go around them, because if we were to knock them out, we would alert them of our presence and we didn't want anyone to know that we had snuck in and out. We weren't taking anything, so there shouldn't be anyone that noticed.

Jack and I had already disrupted the cameras, making them repeat the last hour. We figured at this late of night, the shifts would be the same so it wouldn't have looked odd repeating.

"We need to bounce back and forth between corridors. There are five people in our way. It shouldn't be hard since we know where they are." I pointed at the small map that he had made. "They are here, here, here, here, and here. See what we need to do?"

He nodded. "Yes, I do. Smart thinking and damn, those powers of yours come in handy. Imagine all the trouble we could have gotten in if you had them before now."

"You mean all the trouble we wouldn't have gotten in? I think the missions we were on were troublesome enough. What more could we have done?"

"Well, there's this."

"But why would we have snuck in like this when you were the crime leader of this city? There would be no point."

"For the fun of it."

I rolled my eyes. Only he would think of something so ridiculous. I should have figured. "Let's just focus on the mission, okay? Then when it's all over, when we defeat Nygard, we can do all the missions you want."

He did a little happy jump, ready to get this over with. He was so predictable, but it meant that it distracted him from asking questions and bothering me with them. It had been a while since we worked together, just the two of us. Last time it was with my brother and the others, and the Empire. But this, it was just the two of us.

We ventured down the hallways and I kept my mind open, making sure that we would not run into anyone. I also checked to make sure there was no one reacting from seeing us on the security cameras. Whatever Jack had done must have worked because those people were still in their room, watching the last hour's transmission. Then, in about thirty minutes. it would go back to normal, just a glitch appearing for a moment so that the movement of guards didn't seem so sudden.

"So, what do you think of this place?" Jack asked. "How do you think I could make it better in the future?"

I sighed. Was he really asking me this now? "I think you don't need to worry about making it more secure since you aren't dealing with people that have super powers ever."

"But how do you know that? How do you know there

aren't others out there like Neil?"

"If that's the case, I don't think you should worry about security in this place. I think you should worry that they will take over the galaxy."

Jack shrugged. "I guess that's true."

"Besides, if they would do anything, they would have already done something. So I wouldn't worry about some stupid trophy."

"Just because you don't have to worry about money and goods, doesn't mean the rest of us don't have to."

"Oh, that's right. You're a businessman, aren't you?"

He grinned. "One of the best."

"I don't know, Jack, that Kane seems to be doing a pretty good job."

Jack frowned. "No, he's not. He will fail. At least, that is how history will play out."

"Is there a crime lord that doesn't fail?" I asked. Although I didn't enjoy thinking about it often, the hierarchy of crime lords on this planet changed every decade, or sooner. Jack had been lucky in lasting as long as he did. He was lucky that no one in his circle hadn't killed him in order to gain power.

"There have been a few through the years that have been good and lasted a while. My goal is to outdo them all."

I smiled but didn't answer. It was just a typical response from someone like him. He just wanted to prove himself in the galaxy. Though, then again, didn't we all?

We came upon the room and I took a quick scan

around. The guard that would come by wouldn't be here for another five minutes.

Jack opened the panel to the door and played with the wires. After a couple of moments of tinkering, he looked up at me. "I'll stay outside while you put the gem in the trophy. You have one minute before the lasers turn back on."

I nodded and entered the vault as the doors opened.

There was nothing in here except the three trophies. Seriously, all of this was just for them. It was ridiculous, but to each their own I supposed.

I started for the gold trophy when I stopped. What were the chances I would win first place again? Although I knew I could do it, I didn't want to take that chance. So I stepped to second place and inserted the gem into the base. I secured my mind, not wanting Jack to find out I had put it in third. This was my gem, and I still wasn't sure about Sanshli. I wouldn't let it go to any other person except me. Not even Jack.

Leaving the vault, I grabbed Jack by the hand and we ran before the alarm could sound. I hadn't been on a mission like this in over a year and my adrenaline was pumping. Jack and I had gotten into a lot of trouble together over the years, but this felt like the first time I got to do what I wanted to do without orders issued from higher up the food chain.

We got out of the building with no trouble, but ran straight to the pub, never slowing down. We didn't want to take the chance of being spotted. Laughing, Jack and I stopped in front of the bar.

"It's been so long since I've had that much fun," Jack said.

"Yeah, well, that's because you didn't have me around."

He pulled me in close and kissed me. "Ain't that the truth?"

The smile on his lips faded and Jack looked at the door to the bar, his eyes like a hawk.

"What is it?" I whispered. Then I felt it. There was someone inside the bar. We weren't alone.

He turned back to me. "Cadi, run!"

Suddenly the door opened, and Jack was pulled back. I turned and bolted. Joss had found me. He was fast, he had known where I would go, I should have known. There was still one question in mind.

How did he know that I was at this pub?

Chapter 24

It was still pouring, the storm from the day still continuing on through the night. I let the rain soak my clothes and heard the splash of each puddle as I stepped into it. I knew Tim would follow me. That bastard wanted to catch me at my weakest point, which had always been Jack.

Tim was fast, but I had always been faster. He was the only person I saw, but that didn't mean the others weren't trying to corner me. Who knew, maybe he wasn't supposed to go after me but was always so stubborn that he disobeyed Neil. It wouldn't have surprised me.

I knew these streets like the back of my hands. I knew the ins and outs of where I could go, where I could lose Tim. The only problem was I wasn't sure if I wanted to lose him. I mean, to get out of this predicament, I needed to be captured and get everyone to Sanshli. Then I could be free, or at least that was what I hoped.

The only problem was if I stopped, Tim would use the chance to rub it in my face that he captured me. I couldn't let that happen, now could I?

So my only choice was to run and see if he could catch me.

Rain soaked my clothes now, and I was getting cold. If I concentrated, I knew I could probably take the water off my clothes with my powers, but I couldn't take that much concentration off of running. Tim was right on my heels and if I were to slow down now, he would catch me.

As I ran, I hoped that Jack was okay. I knew if Joss wanted to do anything to him, he would wait until I was there. And I wouldn't let anything bad happen. Not again.

What I always loved about running through the streets of Himeo was the fact that no one noticed. It was like they were so used to people being chased and fights going on that it was no big deal. I didn't know if that was good or bad in this case. I appreciated not being shot at from every direction by either the enemy or officials in the area. But the fact that no one noticed was always disturbing. Especially for one that is used to nothing but action.

I could have sworn that the next right was through an alleyway, leading towards where Jack used to work. Apparently, I was wrong because it was a dead end. Turning around, I found Tim standing in front of me, smiling proudly.

"Shit," I whispered.

He nodded. "Yeah, pretty much."

Before I could do anything, he grabbed me by the throat and pinned me against the brick wall. I felt the brick crack from the force with which he threw me back. I looked at him, his face as wet with sweat as mine. The light from the street cast shadows to where we were, making Tim seem even more frightening. I wouldn't let him have that satisfaction, though. I had to keep my cool.

"Finally caught me, after all these years," I said.

He grinned, his white teeth appearing yellow from the light. "At least your clothes are on this time."

"Watch your tongue, I am mastering my powers."

"Oh yeah," I felt a hot fire on my wrist where his hand was. It seared my skin. "So am I."

Finally, he let the fire subside. It was going to leave a mark, but at least the cool rain felt refreshing on it. I bit back my need to scream out and replied. "Power of fire. Always knew you were hot Thomas, but this is *ridiculous*."

He raised an eyebrow, as if calling him hot was surprising. I should have chosen my words more carefully, but I just wanted to get back to where Jack was. I would say anything to be where he was. "So you admit I'm hot?"

"You were never my type."

"But a crime-infested world with a street boy like Jack is?"

I shrugged. "What can I say, I like what I'm not

allowed to have."

"Speaking of which, Joss is pissed. Better say goodbye to your lover, he's going to kill him for real this time."

I just glared at him. I tried to stay away from weaknesses during my entire Imperial career, yet I had one the entire time. Neil used it to his advantage during that time since he needed me to find Sanshli, now he could do what he always wanted to do: destroy Jack and bring me the pain I deserved for not obeying him as I had promised in the beginning. There was no reason for Joss to keep him alive.

I didn't say a word as Tim brought me back to the bar. I had nothing else to say to him, not after he humiliated me on Anosira. To think I almost… I didn't even want to look at him again, let alone speak any more than we just had. If I could have my way, I would make him eat concrete. However, if I did that, then Joss would hurt Jack and I would be back where I was only a day before, thinking he was dead. Knowing he was dead this time.

How was it always Tim/Thomas who was the one to retrieve me? It had to be Joss' way of putting salt in the wound, making me have to face the fact I had messed up and the one person who I didn't want to boast about how I screwed up was right there to show off. He thought the Emperor saw him as his right-hand man. Unfortunately for him, he didn't realize Joss was using us all. That we all were just puppets in the end.

Then again, he probably liked it that way.

We arrived at the bar and Tim shoved me through the door a little harshly. I thought about kicking him in the leg, but knew that would just end in more petty fighting. Jack was there, being held back by Logan and Jane. Why did he always bring his top people? It was like he had nothing better to do. Jack had cuts on his face, and his nose had blood dripping out of it.

"At last, Myra, I see you decided to show up," Joss said. Dan stood next to him, watching as I glared at Joss and glanced at Jack. "I was wondering if you would come to witness his execution."

"Don't kill him. I will leave him here and do whatever you say. Just let him be." I knew it wouldn't work, we weren't beyond begging. Joss wanted to teach me a lesson. He wouldn't hold back ever again.

"Like I haven't heard that one before Myra." Joss pulled out his Class Two gun and gestured to the guards to make Jack kneel. He pointed his gun at his head. "Say goodbye to your precious crime-lord."

"Jack no!" I screamed as Tim pulled me back.

"Joss stop this now!" Dan ordered. Joss stopped and turned to face him. I couldn't believe what I was seeing. Why would Joss stop just because Dan told him to?

Dan didn't waver. "Let him live. I can't watch Myra suffer like this."

I looked at Dan as if he was crazy. He had no authority over Joss, why would it matter what he said. Dan's appearance changed. He looked as if he was the master, not just some smiling friend as he had always been.

Joss put his gun back into his holster. "Fine, but he will only cause trouble for us and you know that."

I pulled myself out of Tim's grip and ran into Jack's

arms. He held me close. I was so happy that Dan stopped Joss, but I couldn't help but wonder why.

"I don't understand, how did Dan stop Joss?" I asked.

"Because," Jack never let his eyes leave Dan's. "He's the true Emperor. He's Nygard."

I whirled around and stared at him. I could see it now, the resemblance between him and the statue. The statue had crumbled a bit and features weren't as detailed as they used to be. But now I saw Dan in a new light. He was the infamous Nygard.

No, he couldn't be. He was nice, he was kind. He couldn't be that murderer. He couldn't be...

"That means you are..." I began. I couldn't finish what I was saying, I couldn't bear the fact that he was my true father, and my father I had grown to love, the one I cared for, wasn't actually my father.

No, he was. He was more of a father than this person ever could be. I knew that for a fact.

"I am your father, yes," Dan explained. "Sorry I haven't been there for you, I was... indisposed."

"You can read my mind too?" I asked, because that was all I needed.

He smiled. "No, not yours. Your mother made sure of that."

I just stared at him. Had Violet protected my mind from him? When did she do this? Everything was so confusing, and I still hadn't heard a word from her since Anosira. Did it have to do with Dan? Or I guess it was Nygard now.

Jack stood up, his eyes still not leaving Nygard. I

wasn't sure what he would do, but I knew I couldn't stop him. "May I?" he asked Nygard.

Nygard nodded. "Go ahead, be my guest."

Jack smiled and turned to Tim. He punched him in the jaw as hard as he could, which believe me, was hard.

"Jack!" I yelled as I ran to him, holding back his arm as he was about to punch again.

"The bastard deserved it," he said as Tim looked at him, rubbing his jaw.

"I know, but there's one thing you forgot," I said as I turned and punched him myself. This time Tim hit the ground. "I wanted to punch him first."

"Now, reunion aside," Nygard interrupted. "Myra, you stole something off Ttkas. What was it?"

I looked at Jack and back at Nygard. "What do you mean? I told you I was just looking around."

The look Nygard gave me was cold, colder than I had ever seen on his face. Yes, I now knew he was the Sanshlian Emperor, my father, but the moment he gave me those icy cold eyes, I knew that this man had to be capable of anything.

And there was no way I could ever defeat him. Not in any way that I knew.

"I know you took something," Nygard repeated. "I'm not that stupid. What did Violet hide for you?"

I took a deep breath. I had to make this genuine, I had to get him to believe me. Though, it wouldn't be hard. I ran off from Anosira super-fast, not grabbing anything as I left. I had just been lucky that the gem and my pocket watch were on my person.

"It was a gem, it's supposed to show me where Sanshli is. It's still on Anosira, I hid it late one night." I didn't let the lie show through, I knew Joss was reading my mind. He was watching me closely.

"She's telling the truth, at least from what I can tell."

Logan looked the most pissed. "Seriously? We came all the way here for nothing? Damn it Myra."

I couldn't wait until he found out it was actually on Recar all along. He would probably punch me just for the heck of it.

"Well then." Nygard turned to the door. "We shall get back to Anosira immediately."

Chapter 25

"Well that escalated quickly," I commented as the door shut behind Jack. We were in my quarters on Joss' ship. Nygard let us be on the ship not as prisoners, but as regular people. Strangely, he trusted me more than he should.

I rubbed my face, thinking of all that had happened over the past couple days. I started using my powers, thought Jack was dead, found out Jack wasn't dead, hid the gem, got caught by the Empire, Jack almost got killed, my father is Dan who is Nygard, and I almost slept with Tom. It was all too much to handle. Especially the last part.

"How did you not know it was him?" Jack asked. "I mean, he taught you how to use your powers."

"I didn't expect a nice guy like him to be Nygard.

Seriously, he was kind."

"Other than when he shot you?" Jack asked.

I sighed. He had a point. I hated it when he had a point. I should have figured something was up when he would shoot me to coerce me into learning my powers. It made me wonder how he learned his powers as well. "Yeah, there was that. And a few other things." This included how he could teach me my powers, why he was so nice to me, to the point of even worrying about me, and how he could be so good at fighting. He had a lot of years of experience, and perhaps some lingering paternal feelings too.

"It answers everything, doesn't it?" Jack added.

"Stop reading my mind." I swore that if he did it again, I would punch him. I hated it when people kept reading my mind since I didn't know to what extent they were doing it. It was the only thing I had to myself, and apparently, I never even had that.

"I'm not, I'm just making an educated guess. Give me more credit than that. I wasn't the one who didn't recognize their own father," he smiled.

I gave him a look. "Hey, after everything you think it would have been easy for me to recognize him? The only time I ever saw him was when we were in front of that statue, during which my head was swimming in agony. Remember that? I almost went insane."

Wrapping his arms around me, he kissed my forehead. "And I'm glad they are gone, though I'm not sure you losing your sanity would be anything new."

He had a point. I had been through a lot, and I could

break at any moment. "After all that has happened, I'm pretty surprised myself. Especially after being with my brother and Joss all this time."

Thinking of my brother made me think of Lance. I wondered what they were all doing at the moment, if they were searching for me, or if just Lance was. He didn't have anyone to play games with anymore. He was bored and spent all his time in the library.

Jack frowned. "What do you think of Lance?"

"Excuse me?" I asked. He better not be reading my mind or I would be pissed. I could already feel my cheeks turn a little red.

"Just now, you are thinking about him. Why is that?"

I pushed Jack away. "I thought you said you would stop reading my mind. What happened to that?"

"I saw that look on your face and I had to know what you were thinking about. To my surprise, you were thinking about another man."

"It's not like that and you know it. Lance, David, he was the only one who has stood by me after all of this. My brother and Alan would have killed me, and he stopped them. He was my only friend, the only person I could trust would not stab me in the back. That's all." At least that was what I kept telling myself. Honestly, I wondered if my Father hadn't been killed, if our uncle would have still picked up Will and David on Cisum, maybe we'd still have ended up together. I knew it was unlikely, but when I had a year of not doing anything, my mind pondered different hypotheticals.

"You were quick to stab him in the back though."

I didn't know if he meant that in a good way or a bad way. Probably both. "And that's the difference between you and him. I would never do that to you and you know it."

He raised an eyebrow. "You pulled your gun on me on Sanshli."

Right, I had forgotten about that. "Yes, I did, but you knew I wasn't going to shoot you. I wouldn't shoot you, at least not a fatal shot anyway."

Jack laughed. "Oh, that's reassuring."

"You know that's a compliment from me." I let out a sigh and fell on top of the bed. "I don't know what to do next, Jack."

He sat down on the edge of the bed and traced my cheek with his finger. "That's a first coming from you."
I let out a brief chuckle. "I know. This is all so much more complicated than normal. I'm not sure if it's going to turn out how I want it to."

"I think it will. I believe in it, believe that we will win this one."

I shrugged. "So many variables, and now we know Dan is Nygard, I'm not sure I can ever defeat him. I can't even defeat him in hand-to-hand combat, let alone master my powers like that. I don't know what to do."

"We stick to the original plan," Jack said. "I go get Rik and his crew to the races."

"I don't know how easy that will be. We will need to figure out an escape plan and then you will need to convince my brother he needs to get the gem."

"Oh, that can be arranged. Besides, Nygard isn't the one I'm worried about sneaking past. I'm more nervous about Joss. I don't think has stopped monitoring us since we left Recar. He wants us destroyed, but Nygard is too distracted by you to notice me leaving."

I wasn't sure what he meant by that. Nygard had an interest in me, that was for sure. I was his daughter that had been taken from him when he tried to destroy Sanshli. He had killed so many innocent people, yet in person he seemed like a nice guy. I couldn't even think of how it was possible.

But then again, was that where I got my heartlessness? It made sense, really, that he was my father. I had done a lot of the same things he had, killing those who were innocent because they were in my way.

"Why do you think Nygard is distracted by me?" I asked, shoving back the thoughts of being like him. I didn't strive for power, I just strived to survive.

"Are you kidding? He stopped Joss from killing me for you. He had no reason to keep me alive other than to make you happy. His original plan was to never tell you who he was until he gained your trust. He ruined his entire plan for you by stopping Neil. He wanted you to trust him, he wanted you to help him take over the galaxy once again. Doesn't matter though, does it? You trust him and like him, even knowing the truth. You think you are just like him."

"I told you to stop reading my mind."

"Cadi, I'm not, I just know you better than anyone else." He rubbed the scruff on his face. "How can you trust him after all of this? He's the Emperor who destroyed Sanshli! He's the one who brought the Empire into existence in the first place."

"But he's not like the stories, Jack. There has to be more to it. He couldn't have done all of that just for power. He must have had an ulterior motive, a reason he would destroy so many people."

Jack shook his head. "No, he is just acting nice to you because he's a sociopathic freak. Honestly, Cadi, I can't believe you would side with him on this. What are you going to do when we get to Sanshli? You have to defeat him."

"But he's my father."

"Family has never stopped you before," Jack's voice cooled. I glared at him. "Didn't you tell me you killed your uncle? You would have killed Rik too if Sanshli didn't fill your mind. Don't say family matters to you when I know it doesn't."

Jack was irritating me now. He didn't understand what I had been through all this time. "That was different."

"How? That those people were actually close to you? Those people once cared about you while Nygard only wants you to help him gain more power? Or is it that you want that power too, now that you know what you are capable of?"

"Jack, stop it. Now."

Jack went on. "Tell me, Cadi, what makes him different? What makes you not do what you need to do and kill him? We could all go home, safe and sound.

Don't you want to go home?"

"Killing him won't send us home," I said.

He stared at me. "You know that for a fact?"

I nodded. "Yes."

"When's the last time you heard from Violet?"

Jack was pushing me further than he had ever before and it was ticking me off. Was it because of all the time we were apart? Or was it because for once in my life I wasn't walking in a straight line? There was so much going on, I couldn't just decide and do it. I needed to get more details. I stood up and faced Jack. "I said stop reading my mind!"

"Stop letting me. You can block your thoughts. Do it."

I stared daggers at him for a moment longer. This was going nowhere, Jack was just trying to get me angry so I would side with him. It wouldn't work, I needed more time to figure out what to think, who to believe. There was more to this than any of us could have imagined, more to the stories, more than Violet was letting on. The fact was I hadn't seen her since I left Anosira. She had left me and I did not understand why that was. I could get some answers from her, if she was willing, which she wasn't more often than not. Either way, I couldn't believe she would just leave me when I needed her most.

"We need to figure out what to do next."

"Changing topics, you are great at that, aren't you?"

"And you are good at being a selfish ass, but you don't see me pointing that out right now, do you?" I said. He frowned as I went on. "You will need to convince my brother that he can bring back Amanda with that stone on Sanshli, then he will try to get the stone. As for me, I don't think I will have any problem leading the Imperials to Sanshli. Nygard needs to go there to regain his full strength."

"Who do you think will win the races?"

"Me, of course. Is that even a question?"

He shrugged. "I'm just saying it will be a very interesting match, especially with the powers we all possess. The people of Recar will see a show that none will ever see again."

I laughed. "That is true. It will be interesting, to say the least. But before that, we will need to communicate once you leave.

"A way that no one can over hear us, so that leaves out about any communicators."

I tapped my chin. "There may be a way as an illusionist that I can set that up. Mentally calling each other, in a way. Especially if you can read minds already."

"How will you figure that out?"

"Nygard, of course."

Jack crossed his arms. "And how do you think you will figure that out without him being suspicious?"

"I will find a way. Don't worry about that for now."

Chapter 26

It was a six-day trip from Recar to Anosira. Jack and I discussed how we would get him off of Anosira and to Valle. It wouldn't be hard, not when I had the powers of an Illusionist and the fact Nygard kept my training up on the way back. He taught me how to start fires all around and strengthen my skills with using ice, metal, and rock Illusionist abilities. It was all becoming easier and easier with more rigorous practice and I was about to move on up to the more complicated things, things that didn't involve the elements themselves, powers related to the human mind.

An Illusionist, as I knew it, could make a person see anything that they wanted them to see. They could place a person in their worst fear, or their greatest pleasure. Theoretically, I could make someone think they were falling off a cliff, drowning, so on and so forth. I was not sure how I could do just that, but from what I gathered that was the next power that I could possess.

And it felt great.

Never had I thought having so much power over a person could feel good. I always thought power was stupid, that it was the reason there were so many problems in the universe. Never did I realize it could also bring strength to the universe, that if there was enough power held in one spot, one could stop all the nonsense that happened around them. Peace could be achievable.

But that wasn't what I needed to focus on. Right now, I needed to figure out how to communicate to Jack as he was on a different planet at the moment. We needed to stay in touch without having to worry about being overheard.

And the only way to achieve that was to get Nygard to trust me enough to tell me things which he hasn't told me before. I had an idea how that would be accomplished and Jack would not like it, at least if he ever found out.

It was during our sleeping cycle that I went to Nygard's quarters. Jack was out like a light as he was surprisingly a very heavy sleeper for someone always on the alert. If I pulled out a knife or gun on him, he would respond within a fraction of a second by aiming a gun straight back at me. I never figured out if he was actually awake or not.

Nygard answered his door. It was strange looking at

him now. He didn't seem like the same idiotic man that I once knew him as. He was powerful—more powerful than I could ever imagine. And he was my father. A father I never knew yet heard stories about. My life was messed up.

"It's late, Myra, what is it?" he asked.

I took a deep breath. "I had a question for you about training. I didn't want to ask you when Jack was awake in case he overheard us talking."

"Please come in," he waved me inside the quarters. His room was the same as every other room. Gray, bleak, and the only furnishing was a bed and chair.

"So now that I know who you are," I began. "I'm curious about what Joss has told you about me."

He let out a brief laugh. "He doesn't trust you, that's for sure."

"I don't know why, I did everything he has ever ordered of me."

"You also tried to kill him a few times, he has mentioned that."

"He killed my father. Well, my step-father, I guess now. He also tried to kill the person I loved. Yet I killed so many under him and he still doesn't trust me."

"I think it has to do with you loving another man. He never got over the fact you were never 100 percent his."

I didn't want to know what Nygard meant by that. "Either way, he must have had plenty of stories to tell you."

"That he did. All of which I am surprised by. I would think you would take after your mother more than me.

You are much stronger than her, and the heart she possessed is lacking in you as well."

"But you loved her, didn't you?"

He nodded. "I did. Until she betrayed me and took you far away from me. I never thought I would see you again."

"What happened?" I asked.

He sighed and sat down. "It's a long story, one that I will tell you on another day. As for now, you wanted to ask me something, right? Something that not even Jack can hear."

I looked down at my hands, wondering if I would regret my decision. "I was wondering if it was possible to communicate long distances with some kind of spell. Through the mind, of course."

He stared at me for a bit, as if thinking of why I would ask such a thing. "Why do you want to learn that?"

"It was you who put the location of where Jack was in my mind, wasn't it? So I would find him. You have been leading me the way I need to go, teaching me things so I can grow stronger. I think this way we could communicate in situations where you can't be with me, in case I need help."

He rubbed the scruff on his face. "Are you sure? If you do this, it will destroy any spell your mother put on your mind to block it from me."

"She hasn't been there for me when I needed her, she wouldn't teach me the things I needed to grow stronger. So yes, I am sure."

"What did she teach you?"

I was debating whether to answer that. She had warned me about Nygard, everyone had warned me about Nygard, but now that I was face to face with him, I didn't understand how he could be the same guy. He couldn't be the person who everyone made him out to be. "Only how to block people out of my mind, but other than that, nothing."

"Well that will change. You have extraordinary power to stop all of them like you did on Anosira. You didn't even know how you did it, do you?"

"I presumed I thought about time freezing, everything stopping and with such passion I could be stronger. I… liked that feeling of having such power. I want to learn more and I think a communication spell would be helpful in that case."

He grinned. "That's what I like to hear. There is a way for two people to contact using their mind. Only one person needs to be an Illusionist." He gestured to take a seat as he pulled out a candle. "Stuff like this was banned on Sanshli. They didn't want us to gain power to overthrow them. A lot of the spells were lost in the war."

"But you found the book."

"Yes, I did. With it, I could learn many more spells. Ones that weren't illusions. There were beings before us, called the Ancestors. I was able to bring back the original fear that the other Sanshlians had of our kind." He placed the candle on the table. "Let me see your hands."

I held out my hands. He pulled out a knife and pierced both of my middle fingers. Blood dripped down from the wounds. I didn't even flinch. He brought my hands and with each wound, brought my blood from his ear and traced it down to the edges of his mouth, chanting.

"*Quvk vkuh rbaaf, u taccitv eay va pe pucf, pe hayb.*"

I memorized what he said for when I would perform this with Jack. I had to do it like he did, I knew. There wouldn't be a second chance at this.

He brought his bloodied fingers and traced lines from my ears to my mouth. It was interesting how blood was used in this ceremony, whereas the rest of the powers I had been using were in my mind. I wondered how many other spells used blood and to what extent.

"*Ha vkov qi poe tappycutovi vkgaymkay vupi ocf hsoti.*"

He let drops of blood fall from my finger into the candle light. It sizzled as the liquid touched the flame. "Arcadia, repeat after me, '*oc aovk u qubb omgii ysac ycvub u fui*'."

"*Oc aovk u qubb omgii ysac ycvub u fui.*"

The flame grew up, and it felt as if something inside of me turned on. A passage, a connection. I gasped.

I knew I could still hide thoughts from him, of what Jack and I were doing, but it was hard and it scared me. It scared me where he could wander. I didn't let the fear show, but I knew he knew. I could feel it, like a river, as he entered my mind.

And his thoughts entered mine. I could see Violet, and how much Nygard had loved her. He would give anything to be with her, that is until she had betrayed him. I didn't know what to feel about that, as his hatred was beyond anything I have ever felt. Hatred? Maybe it was more like remorse and pain. On top of that, I could see myself as a child. He cherished me more than his own life, that I could feel.

So when Violet took me away, it made him even more angry.

He destroyed so many lives, blood covering everything the eye could see. Even in all my years of being the Emperor's Shadow, I had never seen so much blood. Was this just a glimpse at the power Nygard had? And a better question: was it justified? Did the betrayal of Violet leaving him and how his people were treated justify his revenge?

I didn't know what to feel.

Nygard closed the connection.

"Are you all right?" he asked.

I nodded slowly. "Yeah, I'm fine. It was just," I paused. "Interesting."

"I can only connect with you if you want me to. Remember that."

"Okay, that's good to hear."

"Did I frighten you?"

I shook my head. "No, it was just different. I'm not afraid of you."

"I don't know why, but I don't believe that. But either way, I want you to feel safe. I will not read your mind unless you want me to. And my mind is always open to you. You don't have to worry about me keeping secrets from you. I am an open book, if you will allow it."

I studied him, not sure if he was lying or if he meant what he said. I knew after we landed, after Jack left, I would talk to him about everything that happened. I would find out the truth of what had happened all those years ago. Then I would compare it to the stories I'd been told throughout my life.

"Thank you."

"For what?" he asked.

"For everything. For being honest with me and for teaching me what I need to know. I want to become powerful. I can't stand being weak like I am right now. I can't let people like Tim beat me."

He nodded. "Yes. I will teach you everything you need to know. You will be powerful, just as I hoped you would want to become."

How long had he been waiting for me to say that? How long had he wondered if his daughter would be like him? Was that why Violet wanted me away from him? Because he was powerful and wanted me to be as well?

What was so wrong with being powerful?

I didn't understand why she didn't teach me these things, why she couldn't be the one if she wanted me to defeat Nygard. It made little sense, not to mention I hadn't seen her in a long time. How was I supposed to find her on my own? Everything was unclear, and all I knew right now was that my father was offering me power like I couldn't imagine, power to always be ahead of my enemy.

"I should get back, before Jack notices I'm gone."

"You love him, don't you?"

Another question I wondered if I should be honest about, though after everything it should have been obvious. I nodded. "Yes, I do. I would do anything for him."

"That's what I used to think of your mother. Until she betrayed me. Be careful, Myra, love can blind one's self. I don't want you to suffer the same fate that I had."

"Jack would never hurt me, he would never betray me like that."

He went to open the door for me. As his back was turned, I grabbed a candle to use for the spell. As I stepped out of the room, Nygard looked at me. "That's what I thought. Just be careful, okay?"

I thought about what he said as I walked back to my room where Jack was. Would Jack ever betray me? I doubted it. But after our fight about Nygard, I wasn't sure if he would stay on my side or betray me.

But there was only one way to find out.

Chapter 27

"Did you do it?" Jack asked as I stepped back into the room. I guess he was a lighter sleeper than I thought he was. We were only a few hours from Anosira now, though. It was now or never. If we wanted to communicate without worry, we would have to perform the ceremony at once.

"Yes." I pulled out the candle I had stolen from Nygard's room. "Sit down."

He sat down in front of me. "How did you get him to tell you?"

I didn't answer because I knew what he would say. But it was the only way. I had to do it. "Give me your hands."

He held out his hands. "You let him perform it with you, didn't you?"

I still didn't answer. I pierced his fingers and mine and traced the blood along our cheeks.

"*Quvk vkuh rbaaf, u taccitv eay va pe pucf, pe hayb, ha vkov qi poe tappycutovi vkgaymkay vupi ocf hsoti.*"

Dropping a few drops into the flame of the candle, I had Jack say the same words Nygard told me to say.

"*Oc aovk u qubb omgii ysac ycvub u fui.*" Jack didn't butcher it with his Recarian accent. I was quite surprised, but I didn't show it. The same lucid connection opened up between us. Jack shot up out of his chair. He had a look of fear on his face.

I jumped up. "Are you all right?" For all I knew, it could have been because he wasn't an Illusionist. It could have hurt him and I just didn't realize it.

"I..." he paused. "I'm fine. Just a weird feeling."

I studied him for a moment longer. "As long as you're okay."

"Yeah, this will work great, Cadi." He grinned with the same grin he always gave when he was hiding something. I wasn't sure what that would be, but I decided to not push further. It was apparent he wouldn't tell me.

"So we communicate through this connection. You let me know when you get off this planet and head towards Valle, you got me? Then you get them all to register for the races."

"Of course. I can't wait to cream you on the course."

"I would like to see you try."

"You know how you will distract the rest."

I nodded. "Yes. I know what I need to do."

* * *

We finally landed. The moment we could get off the ship, Joss grabbed me and pulled me into the palace.

"Now where is it?!" he demanded. I just smiled.

"Just wait, it's not going anywhere." I looked at Jack. *Stay in the back, I will take them while you venture off to get a ship. I should be able to make them all still see you, like an after image or a photograph so you can slip away. Let me know when you are ready and are leaving.*

Just as planned? he asked.

Just as planned, I agreed. "I will take you to it. Just follow me." I spun around on my heels and headed down towards the prison cells. It was the furthest point from where Jack would leave. They wouldn't be able to stop him.

As we approached the lifts, as planned, no one noticed that Jack slipped away. And how could they? I had made it so none of them saw it, so none of them noticed that the real Jack had been replaced by a thought in my mind. They believed he was still there. On top of that, they were too focused on me. I was the only one who knew where the gem was, or at least that was what they thought. In actuality, the gem was on Recar and Jack knew where it was.

Well, he knew what room it was. I had switched it into the third-place trophy, just to make sure I would retrieve it and not Jack. I was sneaky that way and I couldn't wait to see his face when he realized it.

Even if Jack betrayed me, if he was persuaded to team up with Wes and give him the gem, Wes would have been able to get it out of the trophy. He could control rock, and the base of the statue was made from granite. He could manipulate it to spit out the gem. Easy as that, other than they wouldn't have the correct trophy.

The elevator stopped, and I realized it had been a long time since I was down here. The last time it had, even when my brother was kidnapped for an assassination attempt on the Emperor and I was interrogating him, ready to put a bullet in my head.

It was where all this chaos had started.

I guess that wasn't true, as the Emperor would have made me go to Sanshli someday anyway. But he needed the clues and only my brother and I could find them, as my father, my Garvnerian father, had left the clues for us. And Violet.

We made it to the room that I had seen my brother tortured in. I would like to see him returned here. He was being an idiot and needed to learn a few more lessons.

"Well?" Joss glanced around. "Where is it?"

Almost out of atmo, Cadi, good luck and I love you. Jack said through our link.

I love you too, Jack. Have fun talking to Wes, your best bet is going through Lance.

And why would that be? Should I tell him you send your love and then punch him in the face?

Of course, he makes such statements as that when we were trying to accomplish a mission. *Shut up and leave.*

"Myra, what are you planning?" Nygard watched me closely. I wondered if he too would open the link between our minds, but I felt nothing.

"Planning?" I smiled. "You mean executing?"

The image I had made in everyone's mind of Jack disappeared. They all searched around for him, but they wouldn't be finding him anywhere near here.

"Myra, where is Jack?" Joss asked.

"Gone," I stated. "On his way to Wes."

"Oh, for your sake, he better not have the gem." Joss got angrier, his face now red. He didn't know how to handle himself around me. I wondered if it had to do now with the fact he didn't have to suck up and worry because I was no longer the key of getting Nygard.

However, I was Nygard's daughter. It wasn't like he could do anything to me without getting in trouble, I now realized. I kind of liked that thought, though it meant Nygard was my father. That part I didn't care for.

"He doesn't," I said. "I wouldn't give the gem to Wes, are you nuts?"

"Then *where* is it?" Joss persisted.

I couldn't help but smile. "On Recar."

Joss looked as if he would strangle me. So did his generals, especially Logan. Actually, I think they had already devised a plan to hold me down and beat the living daylights out of me.

Yet that just made me want to laugh all the more. Maybe I had lost my sanity.

"Damn you!" Joss shouted. "Damn you to the underworld and back!"

"Then we need to head back," Tim commented. "Get to Recar before Jack takes Wes there."

I shook my head. "We don't need to, not right away."

"What do you mean?" Joss asked.

"The gem is in the races' trophy. Only way to get it is to win the races."

"The Recarian races? The same ones I ordered you to win at to get close to Jack?" Joss rubbed his forehead. "Are you serious?"

"Yup. It's a race for the gem. It's in the first-place trophy and if I'm correct, Jack will tell my brother and the others about it as well. So it will be a race." I grinned.

I'm pretty sure Joss was about to strangle me and the only reason he didn't was because my father was standing right there. I figured Nygard would have been pissed, and he too would have punishment in store for me for lying.

But instead, Nygard started laughing. Everyone just stared at him as if he was insane. Though he probably was.

"You used us Myra, just as I would have done." He let the words soak in as he placed his hand on my shoulder. I wasn't sure if he meant it as a praise, or as a threat. "If this is indeed a race, I think we shall start preparing. What do you think?"

Thank you so much for reading! Readers like you make it possible for authors like me to write stories! If you could spare a moment and leave a review on Amazon, Goodreads, BookBub, and wherever you like to buy books, that would mean the world to me! It really helps authors like me to succeed in the publishing world.

A big thank you again for your patronage. I hope you will check out the next book in the series and my other series. Keep reading to get a sneak peak of Book 3 of Sanshlian Series: The Return!

The Return, Book 3 of the Sanshlian Series
PREVIEW

<u>Chapter 1</u>

Three years earlier.

These guys were amateurs.

I glanced back in my rearview mirror to see the next

contestant barely making it around the corner a couple

hundred meters behind me. I licked my lips and smiled.

This was way too easy—I could get used to a life like

this.

The sad part for these guys, I had just learned to drive. I was new to this, and I was still beating them. No wonder the Emperor thought it would be a good idea for me to enter this contest—he had faith I would figure it out.

Taking a deep breath, I tried not to think of what this was really about. I couldn't let my current victory cloud my judgment, as there was a lot at stake here. Although, if I still got second or third in this last race, I would still get first place overall, as my points were exceeding everyone else. But I knew if I let them get near me, someone would try to sabotage my car. I was too good for them, which caused them to resort to illegal tactics.

But that was Recar for you. Legal means accomplished nothing here.

Which was where I came in.

This was my first mission on my own that the Emperor had assigned me. After years of training, I was ready, although I felt I had been ready for awhile now. The mission was to get close to the leader of Recar, Jack McHannon, and assassinate him, as he was causing some trouble for the Pandronan Empire. It was about time the Empire dealt with this planet, and I would be key in that victory. I couldn't wait.

The reason I had to compete in this race, however, was because there was no good way to get close to Jack. He was heavily guarded. However, if I won this race I could become his personal driver. Then I could kill him.

Easy as that.

The Emperor had trained me to stay incognito, but this mission was proving to make that a strenuous task. I was the youngest person to compete, and it was technically against the rules. However, rules didn't matter here, but it was gaining a lot of press and although I tried my best to stay away from cameras by keeping my helmet on as much as possible, those sneaky journalists followed me everywhere and snapped a few pictures. Now everyone knew what I looked like.

I guess I would just be that face everyone feared.

No one knew who I was, but that would change soon. I was the Emperor's Shadow—the person that would be getting the dirty things done. I was to crush any resistance throughout the galaxy. It was what the Emperor trained me to do.

And I didn't have a choice.

I would have been dead if the Emperor didn't find me and adopt me, so to speak. I had tried to kill him a few times, yet he still took me under his wing. Why that was, I did not understand. I tried to bring it up multiple times, but he always ignored the question. I gave up asking him and just accepted my fate—I was his tool.

"Bitch, you better not win this! You aren't even old enough to race! I'm going to—"

I clicked off the radio. Great, they tapped into my car komlink that was only supposed to be used by me and the race coordinators in case there were any hazards or reasons to stop the race. If the man was smart, he would have pretended he was one of the coordinators and created a fake hazard so I would slow down and he could pass me. But instead, as all men like to do, he just threatened me.

I swerved a little right, barely clearing the corner. I needed to keep my mind focused on the race and stop thinking about how stupid people were, and about my past. It was what moved me forward, however, as I had learned to look out for myself and myself only. I didn't trust anyone—I didn't need to. All I needed was myself and I would do anything to keep it that way. I hated working with the Emperor's other generals, as they all wanted to see me fall. They seemed to be jealous of the way the Emperor treated me, although I wasn't sure why. His attention didn't mean I was living a splendid life, it just meant I had more at stake.

Which was why I couldn't mess this up.

Taking a deep breath, I glanced in my rearview mirror again to find one car starting to decrease the distance between us. He must have been using illegal boosters, which were fair game on this planet. It just meant he would lose even harder. I pushed the gas a little more, as he wasn't the only one with a spruced-up engine. The Emperor gave me all the finances I needed to win. I laughed as the car took off.

I still didn't quite understand what the point of these races were. It seemed excessive to have the entire capital Himeo shut down for a week so they could race through the streets. It was all for the leader to decide who would be his next driver. Although the planet was under his rule, there were other bosses in different cities who tried to murder him often. So they needed someone reliable driving him around.

Yeah, this planet was crazy and needed to be ruled under the Empire.

I glanced up at the capitol building to see a figure in the upper window. It was probably Jack McHannon himself watching us race. There was no way to tell, as he was too far up and I had to keep my eyes on the road, but it was a feeling in my gut.

In the past couple of years, I noticed my gut feelings getting stronger and stronger, which has saved my life more than once. I just hoped I wouldn't lose faith in it, or trust it too much, and then be led astray. Intuition could only get me so far in this line of work, yet it was very beneficial. The Emperor said to always trust my feelings when I didn't know what to do next. At first, I didn't understand what he meant, but as time went on, I understood my gut feelings were always right.

The Emperor had taught me everything I knew. Although I had many trainers, it was he who taught me the nitty-gritty, and how to decide to kill someone or to take them in for questioning. Never did I think that would be something I would have to learn after growing up on

Garvner. Now it was all I had to think about. What would my father think of this version of me?

I shook my head. Right now was not the time to think about my father. I had to get him out of my head if I wanted to keep going. I knew in my heart he was watching over me, disappointed in the person I had become. But it wasn't my fault—it was just how the cards fell.

I trained for weeks for this mission—months of almost killing myself in high-speed crashes. I didn't know how to drive before Emperor Neil put me behind the wheel and let me go. All I had ever driven were motorbikes, which I pleaded to race with instead of these stupid cars. They were too clunky and didn't have the same maneuverability. Every time I asked, however, I got slapped. Neil said the races were done with cars because it was all about keeping the leader safe. If he was on a motorbike, he would be a vulnerable target. I disagreed, as there were bulletproof vests and such, but I guess he had a point. I just didn't want to admit it, especially not to him.

Only a few hundred meters to the finish mark. I had this—there was no way I would make any mistakes that would lose me this race.

As if on cue, I heard gunshots fire and hit the back of my car. The second round caused the glass to shatter.

"Sons of bitches!" I yelled back at them, even though I knew they couldn't hear me. I did not have time for this.

I knew I should just ignore it and get to the end of the race, but this was just pissing me off. I pulled out my gun, a TG-2, and pointed it at the bastard who was shooting at me. If he thought he would get away with this, he had another thing coming.

Also, this would show I could fight and race simultaneously. Not that it mattered; I would get the contract, anyway.

I fired three shots straight at where the guy's head stuck out his window. I saw his head jerk back then slump over as his car went out of control and into the barriers. I tried not to think about the people who were standing there watching. Although the streets were supposed to be cleared for this event, some people thought it was a superb idea to stand right behind the barriers and watch, especially near the finish mark. An explosion caused a fiery ball to radiate onto the racetrack and many of the cars either swerved into the other barriers or slammed on their brakes. It didn't matter to me though—I had crossed the finish line.

I had won all the races.

My car came to a stop, and I got out before the reporters could corner me. I ran towards the barrier they weren't allowed to cross, keeping my helmet on. I didn't want more photos of me, especially with what had just happened. My heart was beating fast now, and I could hardly breathe.

Although I had killed quite a few people in past missions, this felt strange. They were just bystanders. Everything felt dizzy. Maybe I wasn't cut out for this. I took a couple of deep breaths and ran towards the bathroom I knew was on the other side of the stage.

Lifting the toilet seat, I threw up.

I heard a knock on the door. "Everything all right, love?"

It was a man's voice. It sounded familiar, but with the

heavy accent many of these Recarian's had, sometimes I just mistook them for another person.

I flushed the toilet. "I'm fine, just got a little car sick."

"It's your first race, right? I don't blame you for getting sick. So many emotions were going through your head, especially when you killed that guy."

I rolled my eyes. Great, that was all that anyone would talk about. I sighed as I rinsed my hands off and opened the door to deal with this guy, who I figured was a reporter.

It wasn't easy to surprise me, but the person waiting outside the door, smiling at me, made my mouth drop. It was Jack McHannon, the ruler of this planet. He had a gentle smile on his scruffy face. He didn't appear to be too much older than me, and it was a wonder how he got to be in his position at such a young age.

"Mister McHannon, I'm sorry, I didn't realize—" I fumbled with my words as too many thoughts were going through my head.

"No apology necessary. I just wanted to make sure my star racer was doing all right. That ending was quite a show, even by my standards. I hope you join my organization after the ceremony. You do have a choice, you know."

I glanced around. We were alone. No one would notice if I killed him right now. I still had my gun on me. It would be easy.

"Yeah, I will join your group. That was the whole reason I entered."

He brushed a piece of my hair back. "That's splendid news. I'm looking forward to spending more time with each other."

I tried not to barf again. Did he think lines like that worked? Although, he wasn't too bad to look at. He had a cocky grin on his face that made a lot of girls smile. I just was not one of them and never would be.

Jack handed me a couple of mints. "Here, for the taste you have in your mouth."

I took them. "Thank you."

"Don't mention it. Now, everyone is waiting for you. Also, keep the helmet off. You have such a gorgeous face."

Maybe I should kill him now. I was getting a little tired of his flirtatious comments. "You are too kind. I'd just rather not deal with the comments some men give me and be recognized for my work, not my face."

"Well, when you work under me, you won't have to worry about comments from people. They won't mess with you once you are connected to me."

I found that hard to believe. "You must have a lot of power over your people then."

"That I do. You will come to find that out soon enough." He held out his hand. "Now, let us not keep them waiting any longer."

As I took his hand, my left hand reached for my TG-2. I could kill him right here and now. Just as I was going to make my decision, a person came around the corner.

Taking my hand off my holster, I smiled.

"I'm looking forward to working with you, Mister McHannon."

Acknowledgements

I want to say thank you to everyone who made this possible. First off, my husband who "gets the pleasure" of reading all my stories multiple times and has always stayed by my side and pushed me forward.

Also, my parents who have supported me since the beginning. To all my friends who get to put up with me talking about my characters, the research I find, and just getting asked the most random questions. Special thank you to my writing group and writing instructors/mentors who have always supported me and believed in me.

Lastly, a special thanks to Justin for always having to edit my work. You are the best! And thank you to Biserka Designs who made a lovely cover!

About the Author

Dani Hoots is a science fiction, fantasy, romance, and young adult author who loves anything with a story. She has a B.S. in Anthropology, a Masters of Urban and Environmental Planning, a Certificate in Novel Writing from Arizona State University, and a BS in Herbal Science from Bastyr University.

Currently she is working on a YA urban fantasy series called Daughter of Hades, a YA urban fantasy series called The Wonderland Chronicles, a historic fantasy vampire series called A World of Vampires, and a YA sci-fi series called Sanshlian Series. She has also started up an indie publishing company called FoxTales Press. She also works with Anthill Studios in creating comics through Antik Comics.

Her hobbies include reading, watching anime, cooking, studying different languages, wire walking, hula hoop, and working with plants. She is also an herbalist and sells her concoctions on FoxCraft Apothecary. She lives in Phoenix with her husband and visits Seattle often.

Feel free to email her with any questions you might have!
danihootsauthor@gmail.com

www.ingramcontent.com/pod-product-compliance
Lightning Source LLC
Chambersburg PA
CBHW070921260626
47162CB00007B/2755